The Plight of a Polish Family

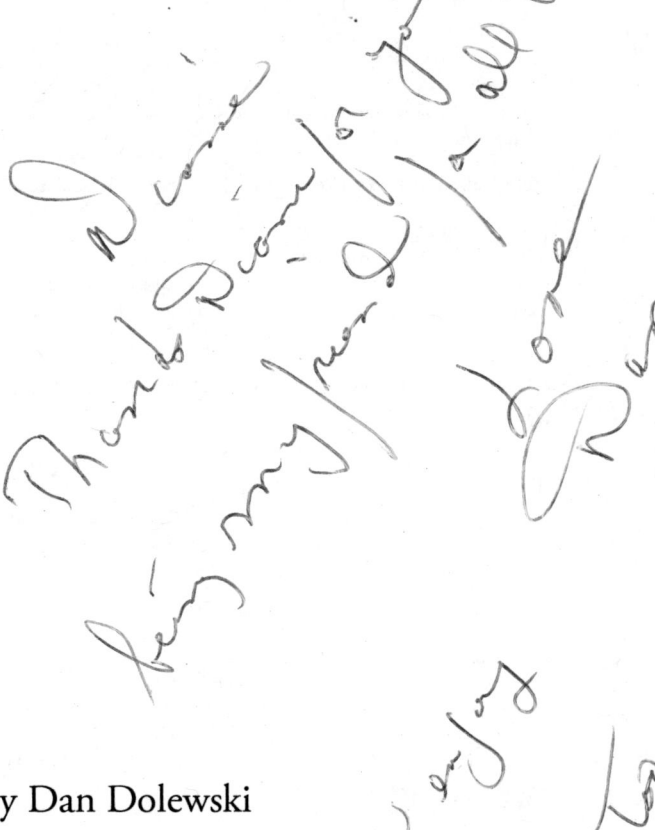

By Dan Dolewski

 www.trafford.com

North America & international
toll-free: 1 888 232 4444 (USA & Canada)
phone: 250 383 6864 ♦ fax: 250 383 6804 ♦ email: info@trafford.com

The United Kingdom & Europe
phone: +44 (0)1865 722 113 ♦ local rate: 0845 230 9601
facsimile: +44 (0)1865 722 868 ♦ email: info.uk@trafford.com

10 9 8 7 6 5 4 3

Special Thanks

To my wife who was my inspiration in writing this book. She died before I could finish it.

To my good friend Frank S., thanks for the help.

To my good friend Diane G., thanks for your typing skill.

To my son John, thank you for your needed help.

To my daughter Linda, thanks for being there.

To my son Dan, thanks for the legal advice.

To Rich P. Suffolk Police Office; Thanks Rich for your valuable input.

To my grandkids for telling me to keep writing.

To all of my friends and family - thanks for your support.

To Cristy Meyer, thank you for your typing skill and reviewing my book.

To Jackie Vero, for the art design of the cover.

Preface

The name of the book I am writing is called "The Plight of a Polish Family", which takes place in the 1930's and goes into the 1950's. The story takes place in a small town in Poland where Mary and John, who are in their 30's, live with their two sons, Steve 18, and Donny 16. Mary's parents also live with them, who the boys call Busia and Dziadzi.

Rumors are everywhere that Germany is getting ready to invade Poland. Many neighbors have already moved, and others are making plans to move. German soldiers have been seen on the outskirts of town, and the boys have run into two soldiers while sledding. One of the soldiers, who they called "Green Teeth", slapped Donny and also hurt Dziadzi because he didn't answer him fast enough.

While spear fishing at lake with their friend, Tommy, they were surprised by Green Teeth, who slapped Tommy to the ground, taking his fish. Steve, holding a six-foot spear, drove the spear into he solder's back.

The family takes a ship to America and settles in a Polish neighborhood in Chicago. Donny has a tough time adjusting to school and gets involved with a bad crowd. Steve gets drafted into the Army and is assigned to a forward observation unit. Donny enlists in the Navy and tries out for the frogmen team. Steve fights the Germans, Donny the Japanese.

Author Information

Dan Dolewski was born in Chicago, Illinois, and at the age of 18 enlisted in the Navy and served in the Seabees. He spent most of his four-year enlistment in Guantanamo Bay, Cuba and one year in Argentia, Newfoundland. He married Marion in 1955 and they have three children: Dan who is an attorney; John who is a Production Control Supervisor; and Linda, who is a Nurse Practitioner. Dan said that his family is the best thing that could have happened to him. He is also blessed with nine grandchildren. Dan's hobbies include oil painting, gardening and reading.

Chapter I

"Good morning, Mom" said Steve as he came into the kitchen. Steve will be 18 in a few more weeks, graduating from high school in June and looking forward to it. He plans to attend the State College for two years, and then go forward and attend a medical college and become a dentist. Right now his plans are to graduate in June and enjoy the summer months. "Wow" he said, "look at all that snow that fell during the night. Do you think we have school?" "I don't know", said his Mom. Why not put the radio on and see".

Just then Donny, the younger of the two boys, came in the kitchen, all excited. Donny is 16, a fun-loving boy. His mother claims that the few gray hairs she has came from him. "Are we off from school, Mom", he asked. "I don't know", she said. "Your brother is listening to the radio to find out". "I sure hope we're off", he said, "so we can go sledding on Suicide Hill." "Hold on a minute", cried his Mom. "What is this Suicide Hill you boys aren't going on"? Steve overheard his Mom and came into the kitchen. "Oh, Mom, it's only a hill at the end of the road. Tommy was showing off and fell off his sled and broke his wrist. Then we named the hill Suicide Hill. Tommy is a very good friend of Steve's. He's a few months older than Steve is, but looks up to him, as do many other boys around.

Mom accepted the story and said, "OK, but first before you boys go out I want you to shovel the snow off the walkway". "Sure thing", said Steve. Donny, who would rather have fun than work, said "Oh Mom, how about we shovel the snow after we get back?" "No way", said Mom. "You either shovel the walkway or stay home". The radio at that moment announced the school closing, and Steve yelled out to Donny, "go to the shed and get the shovels. I'll meet you out there". Donny, still grumbling, put on his coat and rubbers and went out the door.

It didn't take them long to shovel the walkway, with Steve constantly telling Donny to shovel instead of throwing snowballs at him. When they finished, Steve opened the kitchen door and yelled out to his Mom that they are finished and now are going sledding. "You be careful now," cried mother. "Pleases keep an eye on Donny". "I will, Mom", said Steve. Steve was close to his Mom, not like carefree Donny. Mary had a rough time giving birth to Steve and almost lost him. She calls him her miracle baby.

Chapter II

Mary met her husband, John, in college, but didn't start dating him until they graduated and were working at the same hospital. Mary was a registered nurse, and John worked in the admitting office. Once they started dating, it wasn't long after that he proposed. Mary continued working up to the time Steve was born. Afterwards, she worked on a part-time basis. She continued to work until Donny was born, and then became a full-time Mom.

Donny was at the shed, bringing out the two sleds, anxious to get going. "Let's go, Steve", cried Donny, who was walking ahead of Steve at a fast pace. As he approached the top of the hill, he was still in front of Steve. He looked up and saw this huge man who was smiling at Donny. He was showing green teeth and a few missing in front. The man wore a German uniform and helmet. "Hello, Jew boy", he said to Donny, who was startled and said, "I'm not Jewish, I'm Polish". He was starting to tremble now. "Where do you live, little Polack", the German asked. "Down there in town", pointing down the hill. He was shaking so hard now that he wet his pants.

Steve came up to the top of the hill and saw Donny being questioned b the soldier. "And who are you?" asked the soldier. "I'm his older brother", said Steve, trying his best not to look scared. "We came here to sled". Grinning, the soldier said, "I'll ask the questions". "Now I'll ask you the same thing as I did your Polack brother there", pointing at Donny. "Are there any Jews living in this town?" "No", replied Steve. "Only Polish people live here". "I don't know if I should believe you two Polacks", said Green Teeth, "but if I find out that you two lied to me, we will be back and take you two away to a camp you won't like; away from your Mommy". "You understand me, kid", looking straight at Donny. But he was too scared to look up at him. Green Teeth didn't like him not answering fast enough, and took a step toward Donny. He slapped him across the head, knocking his hat off. Green Teeth was enjoying himself and pushed Donny, who fell backwards into the snow. As he was trying to get up, the soldier kicked him in the backside, propelling him down the hill. Steve, seeing that Donny was hurt ran forward and jumped on the soldier's back. Green Teeth was a giant of a man, and easily threw Steve off in the direction of Donny, almost hitting him. Both soldiers were laughing now. Green Teeth looked down at the brothers and said,

"Remember what I told you two, if you lied, we will be back".

As the two soldiers were leaving, Steve got up and went to help Donny get up. "Are you OK," he asked. "Yes", said Donny, "but what in the world are German soldiers doing here?" "I don't know", said Steve. There was a Jewish family that moved into town recently who were middle aged with a 12-year-old daughter. They were very nice and kept to themselves. No one would want to harm them, so why mention it to those soldiers", Steve thought. He looked over at Donny and told him that he was going to go home and tell their Dad about those Germans. "You can stay here with Tommy"', said Steve. "I see Tommy coming up the hill now". "No way", said Donny. He wanted to be the first to tell his parents. The boys started to walk down the hill and met Tommy halfway down. They told Tommy about the incident with the German soldiers, and said that they were going home to tell their parents. Tommy told them that two German solders came to their house early this morning and asked them if any Jewish families live in town. "We told them no, only Polish families live in our town, and they seemed satisfied with our answer because they thanked us and left. Why are they here", asked Tommy. "Who knows", said Steve, "but I sure don't like the looks of it. We will see you later; we have to go now", Steve said. The two brothers left, now anxious to get home.

The snow was deep in spots, and Donny tried to keep up with Steve, but kept slipping in the heavy snow. He got up and tried to run but fell backwards, rolling into a snow back. Steve saw him lying there and went to his brother's aid. "What's the matter, little brother", he said. "I'm out of breath", cried Donny. "You go ahead and I will see you at the house". "OK", said Steve. "Take some time and relax", he said as he started down the hill.

The house was just around the bend now, so he started running a little faster. A few seconds passed, and Donny was up on his feet, brushing the snow off his pants and eager to get going to catch his brother, who now was out of sight. Donny started to run faster, but slipped again and went down on all fours. He jumped back to his feet, but decided to give up trying to catch Steve, and started to walk down. Steve rounded the bend and focused his eyes on his house. He caught a glimpse of his father kneeling in the snow, holding someone in his lap. Were his eyes playing tricks on him, he thought. As he got closer, he saw his Dad holding his Grandpa.

Busia and Grandpa, or Dziadzi as they called him, have been living with them for as long as Steve could remember. Grandpa was bleeding from his hand, and it was swollen and bluish in color. "What happened to Dziadzi", cried Steve. "Two German solders came by and asked Dziadzi is any Jews lived in our town. Dziadzi had his hand on the pole, trying to get up and ignored the soldier, and the other one raised his rifle and came down with the butt on his hand". Donny arrived just then and was told the same". "You boys will have to help me get him into the house". They got Grandpa on the sled, and while their Father held him, they pulled the sled with the rope that was attached. As they got nearer to the house, Busia and Mary came running toward them. John explained what had happened, and they all helped Grandpa into the house and then into bed. Busia told the boys to go get Dr. Adamski who lived three blocks away. The doctor was a very dedicated man in his 50's. They covered Grandpa with blankets to keep him warm.

Chapter III

Busia was a nurse in her earlier years, but gave it up when Mary was born. Dziadzi was a good businessman. He got his start by selling screws, nuts and bolts. He built up his business in a short time to take care of two towns. People came from miles away to buy hardware from him.

Dr. Adamski arrived with the boys and was shown to where Grandpa was laying in bed. The doctor proceeded to examine him and told Mary and Busia that he should be taken to a hospital where he could get better care. Busia disagreed with him and said that Dziadzi would never consent to going to a hospital. He always said that hospitals are for the dying. Grandpa is 84 years old and a very proud man. "Well", said the doctor, "all I can do for him then is to clean the wound, bandage it, and give him medication for pain. "He may require surgery on that hand later on", the doctor said. He then bandaged the hand and told Mary to call him if he is in severe pain. She thanked him and he left.

"Mary", said John, "we have to get out of Poland as soon as we can, before that little dictator arrives with his troops in our town. I can't understand how this country allows those Nazis to walk around and do whatever they want". Donny, who was in the living room, walked into the bedroom where everyone was and asked his Dad if the soldier who did this to Grandpa had green and missing teeth. "Yes", said his Dad, "But how did you know? You weren't there". "We saw them up on the hill and they asked Steve and me if any Jews live in our town. We told them no, only Polish families. I didn't think Green Teeth liked the way I answered him, because he slapped me in the head, and then kicked me as I was trying to get up. Steve jumped on his back, but he threw him off, down the hill, and they told us that if we lied to them, they would be back and take us away from you and Mom". "Those rotten Nazis", cried John. "No one is going to take you boys away from us", he said. "That's it, Mary. Tomorrow I'm going into town and see when the next boat leaves for America".

The next day when John asked about booking passage aboard the boat to America, he was told that no boats would arrive or sail until the ice melts in the harbor. "It could be two months away", he said. John purchased the tickets and hoped for warmer weather to come.

John and Mary had very close friends living in America, Joseph and Eleanor Manowski. They were like family, godparents to Steve. The boys called them Uncle Joe and Aunt Eleanor. They were neighbors for years, and spent most of the holidays together. They got worried that the Germans were getting too big and feared that they would soon invade Poland, so they packed up and sailed to America. They now lived in Chicago in a Polish neighborhood. They wrote constantly and asked Mary and John to move there.

Chapter IV

Joe and Eleanor told Mary and John that if they plan to move to Chicago, they can have the full second floor of their house to live in. This includes two bedrooms, a large living room, a large dining room, an eat-in kitchen, and a large bathroom. The basement has a large store that will be vacant soon, and John could set up his business there. "I'll write them today", said John, "and let them know of our plans. "I'll start packing some of our things", said Mary. John interrupted her and said, "Now don't go packing everything! I know you too well. If you could, you would pack the nails holding down the rugs"! "Oh John, stop exaggerating", laughed Mary. "Well then", said John, "we can buy anything we forgot in Chicago".

John and Mary will be married 18 years soon, and Mary said it would be great to celebrate their anniversary with Joe and Eleanor in Chicago. "We will, honey", said John. The weather turned warm, and each day a little warmer, so John took another ride into town to check on the ship's departure. He was told that if the harbor continues to melt with this warm weather, the guess would be that the ship could leave in two weeks. "Continue to check with us", said the dock master. When he got home to tell Mary, the two of them got all excited and started dancing around the kitchen. "It won't be long, Mary", he said.

John and Mary were well known in town. Grandpa and John opened a hardware store and were doing well. Busia and Steve helped out whenever they could. Grandpa would not let Steve's schoolwork interfere with his working. "School always comes first", he would tell him. Everybody said Grandpa and Steve got along like two peas in a pod; they know it, too. When things slowed down in the hardware store, John enrolled in a class at school to learn the furrier business. He did well at it and soon mastered the profession. He made winter coats for Mary and Busia that were the envy of the women in town. He now knew what he wanted to do for a living.

Grandpa took a turn for the worse. His temperature flared up, so Mary called the doctor who came over in less than an hour and found Grandpa trying to sit up. But he was too weak to do so. The doctor stayed until Grandpa's temperature broke and he was cool again. Before he left, he told Mary to call him if his temperature should fire up again. Grandpa was improving daily, and started to talk about going back to work. He said that he would put his arm in a sling if he had to. This made Mary and Busia happy.

A week went by and Grandpa was getting dressed when he suffered a massive stroke. Mary heard him hit the floor and rush into the room to find him on the floor. She called the doctor who rushed right over and confirmed her fears that Grandpa was dead. The family took it hard, especially Busia, Mary and Steve, who was Dziadzi's favorite. "Dziadzi was looking forward to going to America", he said in tears. Many friends and neighbors came over to pay their respects.

Three weeks went by after Grandpa's burial, and Busia got the family together. She said, "Dziadzi would want us to continue our plans to go to America. He wouldn't want us to mourn him for this long. Busia was the monarch of the family. "The first thing we have to do", said Busia, "is to sell the hardware store. The money we get from the sale will go for your new store in America, John". They had been getting a lot of offers for the store. Busia said, "I will contact these people now and see if they are still interested". A few days passed, and Busia got a handsome price for the store. She was also a smart businesswoman.

The warm weather continued, and it was beginning to feel like a heat wave, with temperatures going into the 80's. The boys quickly got into their bathing suits and headed for the swimming hole, a fresh water lake surrounded by big bushes and trees. This was a favorite spot for the boys. They felt like it all belonged to them, since they took care of it. Not many kids knew about this spot. They usually went to the beach. The boys enjoyed that, and they built themselves a raft out of wood that Grandpa gave them, and used it to go fishing. Instead of using fishing poles, the boys cut up tree limbs and sharpened the points. They made ten spears and cut them to five and six feet long. They would row the raft to the middle of the lake where the water was six feet deep and crystal clear. They then would put the spears in the water and wait for the fish to swim by. Their favorite fish was the Catfish. They were big and slow and easy to spear. They would spear five or six when they would go out. Mary would blacken them, and they tasted better than chicken. They would have fish two or three times a week. The whole family looked forward to it. In the winter months the boys would cut a hole in the ice and spear the fish. They kidded one another and called each other Eskimos.

Kielbasa, which was polish sausage, was usually cooked for the holidays. Mary would make her own sausage. Busia was the expert on stuffed cabbage, called golumpki, and was the family's favorite. Here again, no one made anything as good as Busia, with Mary assisting. John loved to come home and smell the Bobka and other things n the oven. He kept sampling things in the oven. Busia loved John and always made a small piece for him.

The weather continued to stay warm, and the ice in the harbor was melting fast. John took a ride into town to check on the ship's departure, and was told that, if the weather stays this warm, the ship should leave in one week. "OK", said John. He felt like doing a dance.

After school it was still warm, so the boys went to the lake to cool down. They picked up Tommy on the way. When they got to the lake, Tommy said, "How about going fishing to cool off"? "OK by me", said Steve. "How about you, Donny"? "No", said Donny. "I would rather go swimming than go on the raft and roast in the hot sun". "OK", said Steve. "We should be back in an hour or sooner". "Don't rush back on my account", said Donny. "I'll be cooling off in the water while you guys will be sweating". Steve told Tommy to get the spears while he put the raft in the water. Tommy left and in a few minutes he was back with two six-foot spears. "Let's go", he said. He and Steve pushed the raft into the water. They rowed to the middle of the lake. It was the boys' favorite spot. The water was crystal clear; you could see clear to the bottom. They seldom went further than around the bend where the water was very deep and murky. The weeds were heavy, coming up to the top of the water. It wasn't long before Steve speared his first catfish. By the time Tommy got his first fish, Steve speared his second. They got a total of four fish, and then decided to go back and do some swimming. They were hot and getting sunburned.

Back on the beach, Donny was swinging on a rope tied to a tree. The boys would propel themselves into the water and see who could go the farthest.

At home, Mary and John were going over their finances and trying to figure out what to bring on their trip. While they were in college,

John was known as a "ladies man", but he did not date much. Mary was pretty, religious, blue-eyed brunette with a knockout shape. She was also a terrific tennis player, and was on the tennis team, as was John. On their first date, they played tennis, and John felt as if Mary had let him win. They were voted King and Queen in their last year of college. They were married soon after college. They talked about having a large family, but it did not turn out that way.

The boys enjoyed racing each other, with Tommy winning most of the races. Both boys gave him competition. Donny would swim into Tommy at times to give his brother the edge and the win. Tommy would just shrug it off and not argue about it, knowing Donny's intentions to help out his brother. Tommy was considered a great friend.

As Donny swam to shore, he was startled to see Green Teeth, waving him to shore. "Come on, Polack", he yelled. Donny's first thought was to swim out to deeper water, but he saw the rifle in the soldier's hands and started to swim to shore. As he got closer, Green Teeth waded into the water to meet him, and grabbed Donny by his arm and jerked him out of the water, hurting him as he did so. "Where is your brother", asked the soldier. "Out there", Donny said, point down toward the lake. "He's fishing. Why?" Donny looked around for the other soldier, but he was nowhere to be found. The soldier said, "We will wait for your brother". Again Donny asked, "Why?" "Because I said so, " said Green Teeth.

Jus then Steve and Tommy came onto shore and were approaching them. "Hey let me have those fish", said the soldier, extending his big hand to the boys. "No way!" cried Tommy.

Chapter V

"We worked too hard to get these fish", he said, and slowly started to back away. Green Teeth took a step forward and said, "Is that so?" and hit Tommy across the face with his fist, knocking Tommy to the ground. The soldier then reached down to grab the fish when Steve rushed forward with the spear in his hand and plunged it into the soldier's back. Green Teeth opened his mouth to scream but no sound came out, just a stream of blood. Steve removed the spear and plunged it into him again, breaking the spear as it hit the soldier's chest bones. Steve backed away as the soldier fell forward, close to where Tommy was.

Donny, who was watching all this, was shaking on the ground and started vomiting. "Stop it, Donny", cried Steve. "Don't you remember what he did to you and Grandpa on the hill?" Donny looked up at Steve, but could not look in the soldier's direction. "OK", said Steve. "When he doesn't report back to his barracks tonight, they will start searching for him. That means we have to bury his body and get rid of all the evidence. I want you two to go back to the house and get two shovels and start digging a hole over by the bushes there", Steve said, pointing to the tall bushes near the end of the beach. "No one can see you digging over there. While you're doing that, I will load up the raft with his rifle, bayonet, and helmet and row out to the deep end of the lake and dump them there so they will never be found. When I get back, I will help you guys dig".

"OK", said Tommy, and the two left. Donny kept thinking about the other soldier. Why wasn't he around? "I sure hope he isn't here", said Tommy. They then started to run. Steve loaded the rifle, bayonet, helmet, and the soldier's canteen on the raft, and then proceeded to row to the deep end of the lake where the water was murky and full of seaweed. A good place to dump the soldier's equipment. He dumped everything in the water, and watched it vanish in the seaweed. Never to be found, he thought. Steve then started to row back to the beach to help Tommy and Donny.

They all took turns digging, and when the hole was deep and wide enough, they dragged the dead solder's body to the hole and dumped him in. They then covered the body with dirt and sand. They stomped on the ground and added sand and leaves on top. The final touch was to throw some twigs, tree limbs and other debris around the top. Steve checked the grave and gave his final approval. They threw sand around where the body lay, covering all the blood with sand. "High tide will wipe it clean", said Steve. "Now let's all go home", he said.

On the way home, Steve said that no more of today would be brought up. They all agreed, and shook hands on it. In a few days we'll come back here and check to see if there is any seepage of dirt on the grave. The dirt will settle and maybe show a little, so we will have to fill in the dirt. We may be watched, so we have to be extra careful from now on. When we come back here we just can't go to the grave. What we'll do is come here, like we always do, and will go right into the water, swim around for a half-hour, and then come out and start playing tag. You can chase me, Tommy, and I will head for the grave. Just before you tag me, I'll fall in front of the grave, and you jump on top of me, at the same time looking for any seepage. We throw the dirt around in case we see any loose dirt around, and then get up and head for the water, without raising any suspicion or being obvious, right? After we leave for America, you may want to come over here and check from a distance, Tommy. "Right", said Tommy. "Boy, I sure will miss you guys", he said. "I wish you were coming with us", Steve said. "Maybe someday", he said.

John once again took a ride into town to check on the ship's departure. He was told that the ship would leave in five days. He was handed a stack of labels, and was told to label any furniture he was taking to America. Start bringing down the furniture to the dock starting tomorrow, he was told. Be ready to sail on Monday.

When he got home, he asked his neighbor who had a truck, if he could start bringing his furniture to the pier. "No problem", said his neighbor. "Just make sure everything is labeled, John", he said. John couldn't wait to tell Mary. Steve and Donny could help him load, he thought. Most of the packing was complete; now all they had to do is label everything.

Two days passed, and Steve told Donny that they would have to go to the lake today and check out the grave for scepage. "OK", said Donny. "I'm ready to go". On the way they picked up Tommy and made their plans. Donny would go into the water while Steve and Tommy would work on the raft, then play tag. He told Donny not to look suspicious or look in their direction, in case they are being watched. They picked up Tommy, and again went over their plans. When they got to the lake, Donny ran right into the water while Steve and Tommy took the raft out and examined it as if looking for problems. After a few minutes, Steve tagged Tommy and started his run toward the grave. Tommy was a few feet behind him. When Steve got by the grave, he glanced down, looking for any seepage or any indication of a grave. Seeing nothing, he slipped to his knees with Tommy on him. They rolled around the sand. Steve was satisfied everything was normal, jumped to his feet and started after Tommy who was heading for the water. When they got to the water, Steve tackled him and they both went under, enjoying the comfort of the cold water. They swam around for a little while, and then joined Donny, who was ready to go home. Donny asked Steve how everything was and if the ground had settled much. "No. We did a good job of it. You can't tell at all". He looked over at Tommy and said, "In a month or so, go back there and look around, but don't make it obvious, OK?" "Right", said Tommy. They all felt pretty good now, knowing Green Teeth will never be found.

Chapter VI

When the boys got home, they saw their father moving all the furniture. They all helped him and spent the rest of the day loading the neighbor's truck and bringing it down to the dock. Donny and Steve were excited now, their first trip on a ship.

Monday came, and all the furniture and things they were bringing with them were on the ship. The ship was to sail at noon, and they had a beautiful warm sunny day to sail on. A neighbor took them to the ship, and they boarded, anxious to get going. Many of their neighbors came to the dock to wish them a safe journey. Mary, John, Busia and the boys were standing on deck, waving to the neighbors. Mary was crying, as were the neighbors on the dock. "We are leaving a lot of good memories behind, John", said Mary, grasping Busia and John's hand. "A lot of memories, indeed", said John, "but a great future in store for us in America. A place where we don't have to worry about wars, a place our children can grow up in peace. "I know", she said, as she grasped his hand tighter. He just smiled back at her. As the ship was pulling out, everyone was waving, until they no longer could see the dock.

The first two days at sea were very calm, and they had lifeboat drills and were assigned lifeboat stations. No mention of the German subs was ever mentioned, because they weren't at war yet.

On the fifth day out, the passengers were told that they were heading into a fast approaching storm. Pails were handed out in case they got sick. The storm may last a day or two, they were told. John and they boys weren't that concerned about getting sick, but Mary was very concerned. Her stomach was queasy already. The storm hit early in the evening, right after dinner. The ship rolled and pitched most of the night, and most of the passengers, including Mary, were sick. Breakfast was missed by most of the passengers, but John and the boys ate, bringing fruit and crackers to Mary. Mary sat in her bunk, as did most of the passengers who were seasick. It seemed like the only remedy. John helped Mary up on deck, when the sun came out and the water became calm, Mary ate dinner for the first time in two days. Most of the passengers were up on deck, enjoying the calm sea and the sunny, warm air. "I sure hope we don't run into any more storms", she said. "I hope not", said John. He was happy to see Mary feeling good again.

They had nice weather for the rest of the trip and spent a lot of time on deck. They met a family who lived near their town and shared stories with them. They spent time playing shuffleboard and cards with them. They were on their way to New York to live with their in-laws. They had mixed feelings about leaving Poland, but with the War in the wind, they thought it better to leave before they were caught up in it. "We hope we made the right choice", they said. John told them about their experience with the two German soldiers. John believed he convinced them that they did the right thing. They told John that they were Polish Jews.

While at sea, the passengers were told that Hitler had invaded France. Rumors started flying aboard ship that Poland would be next, and then what? The Polish Army was no match to the German armor and trained troops. "What chance do we have with our cavalry against their tanks", said John. When the boys heard about it, Steve said to Donny, "Well, there will be one less German that won't kill any Poles". "Yea", said Donny. The boys started to wonder what would happen to Tommy and his family if the Germans go into their town.

When the Germans did come to town, they rounded up all the young, healthy and strong-looking men and put them on trains. The destinations were places that the Germans were laying rails for the trains that would carry supplies to the front lines. Tommy and his Dad were in that group. Tommy's mother was a nurse by trade, and was taken to a hospital to take care of the German soldiers. All three survived the war and in 1945 they reunited near the German border. They went back to their old town, which they found to be almost leveled by the bombings. Their home was no longer there, and they just looked at the spot where it stood and cried. They would rebuild their house, as did other old neighbors who came back. John and Mary's house escaped most of the bombs and was partially standing. The hardware store wasn't as lucky, and was demolished.

The ship approached the New York harbor and slowed down. Most of the passengers were up on deck now, watching the tugboats slowly bringing them to the dock. They would now have to go through customs and immigration, which would take the rest of the morning. They planned to ship all their furniture to Chicago; to the address Joe gave them. The train ride to Chicago was a real joy for them, looking at all the towns they passed. The boys had their noses almost against the windows.

When they arrived in Chicago, they were met by Joe and Eleanor, who was carrying flowers for Mary. "Thank you, Lord", John was heard to say as he got off the train and walked into the depot. The boys were the first to see Joe and Eleanor and yelled out, "Look, Mom and Dad, there's Aunt Eleanor and Uncle Joe". They were upon them in a second, and then all the hugging and kissing started, going from one to the other. Steve and Donny got all choked up, too. After all the hugging, hissing and crying, Eleanor said, "Thank God you left when you did. There is no contact with anyone in Poland since the Germans invaded in full force. We were told that our armies put up a gallant fight, but were no match for the German army and their tanks. We don't even know what happened to our parents and wonder if they could have survived the onslaught. No one has any information". "Has America entered the war", asked John. "No", said Joe, "but England has. Roosevelt was on the radio last night and said that he would send supplies to England but would try to keep America out of the war as long as he can. America wants peace", he said.

Finally, after a long day, they were on their way to their new home. "Once you are all settled, John, I will teach you how to drive", said Joe. Their apartment consisted of three bedrooms, a large kitchen, dining room, bathroom and living room. They also had a porch to sit on during the hot summer months. Downstairs is an empty store that can be used for business. "We can look at it tomorrow. It has a few things in it that I'm sure you will be able to use". John was getting excited now and eager to look at the store. Joe told John that the guy who rented the store before ran a cleaning and tailor shop. "He was fine for awhile, but his marriage fell apart, and he started drinking heavily. He owed me rent money, and he moved to Florida. Before he left, we made a deal that he would leave everything in the store behind for the owed rent". Joe said that he felt like he did OK on the deal. All the furniture would be arriving in a few days. The boys would share a bedroom that had bunk beds in it. "I'll take the top bunk", said Donny. "OK", said Steve, as the two went back to looking out the window.

Tomorrow, Mary, you and I will go to the mall shopping", said

Eleanor, "while the men talk shop". "OK by me", said Mary. "I can't wait to see all those stores you mentioned in your letters. I have so much to ask you about Chicago. Could we stop and see that church that is close by"? "Sure", said Eleanor. "We will shop and have lunch at the mall and I'll try to bring you up to date on all the sights I'm sure you will want to see". "Great", said Mary.

After the women had left, Joe and John went downstairs to see the store where John has planned to set up his business. John looked at all the equipment left in the store by the last tenant. In one corner of the store was a presser machine operated by steam for large objects to iron. Next to this machine was a large ironing board with a large iron. John lifted the iron and was surprised at how heavy it was. A sewing machine was near the front door. A row of hangers on a pole was on one side, and a gigantic glass closet full of hangers was against the left wall. The closet had glass doors on it. It smelled from mothballs. This is where the fur coasts and other items needing storage during the summer months, thought John. He could picture the closet full of fur coats. The store had a big picture window in it and John looked at Joe and said "John the Furrier and Tailor". "I like the sound of it", he said. "The sign will be first on the list", said Joe. "I'll contact the man this afternoon", he said.

Chapter VII

John was anxious to get started in his new venture. He felt he would do well here. He had leaflets printed out that told of his new store opening. There weren't any tailors or cleaners in the vicinity, let along a furrier. He felt very good about this, and was ready to meet the challenge. The boys passed out the leaflets to all the homes in the neighborhood. The grand opening was scheduled in two weeks. John felt confident that he would be ready.

Donny was having a hard time adjusting to school. He started hanging out with a bad crowd. Steve got wind of it and told Donny to break away from them, but Donny just shrugged him off. The leader of the group was called "Birdie", a short pimple-faced boy of 17. Donny liked him and went along with whatever Birdie said. He was being used, and Birdie enjoyed his newest follower.

One day at gym class, the teacher told the boys that they would go out today and play softball. Donny was a natural when it came to sports, especially baseball. Softball in Chicago was played without gloves, and a 16-inch ball was used. Ten men to a team. Birdie was impressed with Donny's playing ability and after the game came over to Donny and said, "I'm putting together a softball team and could use you on my team". Donny felt good that Birdie was paying attention to him. They practiced every day after school.

Birdie got a game with one of the teams practicing at the park. He watch them practice for a while and figured his team could beat them. He booked the game for a night game under the park lights. It was nice playing under the lights. Donny never experienced that before. A small crowd showed up to watch them, mostly girlfriends of the boys on the other team. They played well, but the other team got lucky in the late innings and beat them 7 to 5. Birdie was all upset; he was a sore loser. As they were leaving, he called out to the other team that they would be back to have a rumble. "So be prepared', he told them. Donny heard him, but couldn't understand the reason he said it. When they got back to the candy store that they spent a lot of time at, Birdie picked up a few of his friends, a bunch of toughies that hung out at the store. They all got in Birdie's pickup truck and were all set to rumble. The other boys didn't want any part of them. Donny wasn't sure he wanted to go, but Birdie called out to him to jump in the back, and Donny did as he was told. He didn't want to be called a chicken or to offend Birdie.

When they approached the park, one of the boys in the back yelled out that a police car was following them. Birdie started to panic because he had a blackjack in the glove compartment, and told the boy sitting next to him to get it out and put it behind him on the seat. The police put their lights and told them on a loudspeaker to pull over, which Birdie knew he had to do. They were told to get out of the truck and told to sit down on the lawn. The police found the blackjack under the front seat, and called for a meat wagon, a police van used to transport prisoners.

The van came a short while later, and they were all told to get in. The van had two steps in the back to get in. It had a row of wooden benches on either side, and when the door slammed shut, there were bars across the door. Donny felt like a common criminal, embarrassed more than scared. As they got to the police station, Birdie said, "Now don't forget, nobody knows whom the blackjack belongs to". The ride took fifteen minutes, and as they arrived, they were taken to a holding cell, a large room with wooden benches to sit on. Each boy was taken out and questioned about the blackjack. They all said that they knew nothing of the blackjack. They were held for another hour and then told to call their parents to pick them up. Donny called his Uncle Joe because their phone wasn't hooked up yet. He pleaded with him not to tell his parents, and he said he wouldn't He picked him up and was told that he would have to appear in two weeks with Donny in front of a judge. Joe told him that he did a bad thing, but would appear with him in court and try to keep it from his parents.

Steve found out about it from the boys in the neighborhood and told his parents about it. All heck broke loose. Joe was relieved that it was out in the open because he didn't know how long he could keep it from Mary and John. Donny received the silent treatment from the family, after he was told they were ashamed of his being arrested. Donny wished his Dad would yell or hit him or punish him in some way. Steve laced into him and told him to drop Birdie and stop being his whipping boy. "You don't need him", he said. "He's just using all of you guys". "Yea", said Donny. "I'm learning the hard way.

Donny didn't like the silent treatment he was getting at home. He wished his parents would yell at him for being stupid, and then get on with it. He knew he deserved this type of punishment, but wished it were over with. "What's going to happen to me when I get in front of the judge", he thought. He just had to sweet it out; that's the hard part. The next morning, after a miserable night's sleep, he made himself breakfast and went on his way to school. He felt like everyone was looking at him in class, and he felt uneasy. He ran into Birdie in his gym class. "Hey buddy, how are you doing", he asked. "Not too good", said Donny. "My parents are giving me the silent treatment". "I'm sorry to hear that", Birdie said. "Hey, good buddy, you have to do me a favor", said Birdie. "You're the youngest guy in my gang, and when we go up before the judge in two weeks, I want you to tell him that it was your blackjack. He will go easy on you; with me, he won't go easy, seeing that I spent time in reform school and was in trouble after that. You have to bail me out on this, OK, good buddy?" "I'll see", said Donny, and went to his locker to put on his gym clothes. All day Donny kept thinking about what Birdie had asked him. "It's not fair for him to ask that of me", he thought.

Chapter VIII

The day finally came for Donny to go to court, and he got all dressed up in his blue suit. The whole family was going with him, which he was glad of. When he went to the seat assigned him, he saw Birdie look at him, smiling and giving him a thumbs-up gesture. All the boys were being called up before the judge and asked if they knew whom the blackjack belonged to. They all said no. Donny was called in front of the judge and asked if he knew whom it belonged to. He said, "Yes I do. It belonged to Birdie", pointing him out. Birdie's mouth flew open as if to say something, but nothing came out. Donny proceeded to tell the judge that Birdie asked him to say it was his, but he said he couldn't do that. The judge thanked him and said he felt as if Donny would do well in his adult life. Mary and John came up to him and hugged and kissed him. Steve told him he was proud of him. When Birdie got before the judge, he was given a six-month jail sentence. Donny never heard from Birdie again.

Birdie was released after serving three months in jail, and a week later was robbing a grocery store and was shot dead by the owner of the store. Donny went to the wake, only because he felt sorry for Birdie. Not too many attended the wake; not one person from Birdie's old gang was there. Birdie's mother and sister thanked Donny for coming. As he left, he felt good about himself for going.

John's business was picking up new customers daily. He started to take in cleaning, which helped the business. The closest cleaner was two towns away, and being in a Polish neighborhood made it so much better. A factory cleaner would come by every Tuesday with a van and pick up the clothes to be cleaned and deliver them back by Friday morning, giving John the weekend to iron the clothes and have them ready for the customer early in the week. The only drawback was that most of his Polish customers came over to chat with John. Whenever any news came to them about Poland, John would be the second person to hear about it. Mary told him the shop looked like a Polish meeting place. At times he would have to work late into the night to catch up on his work. He always tried to keep his customers happy and have their clothes ready for them.

Sundays were usually a day of rest. In the summer when it was hot out, they would take a bus down to North Avenue Beach, which was only forty minutes from them. Mary would pack a lunch of southern fried chicken, salads and soda, and they would spend most of the day there. The boys and John would swim, keeping cool, but Mary would enjoy herself sitting on a blanket and watching her family playing in the surf. Sometimes on a Sunday or holiday, they would go with Joe and Eleanor to a lake nearby, or once in a while take a trip to Lake Geneva, which they all loved. But it was a long trip, which took close to an hour and a half. They went there on special occasions. Some of the lakes they went to reminded Mary of the lakes she went to in Poland. Only then did she start feeling homesick for Poland, but all she had to do then is to look over at John and her two boys and she felt better.

John wasn't into sports like his boys, but Joe was. On occasion, Joe would take the boys to Wrigley Field to watch the Cubs play. If you lived in Chicago, you were a Cubs fan. The boys loved going to the ballpark, especially early so they could go down to field level and get autographs. Steve got Stan Hacks and Phil Cavertta's in one day. Donny got Clyde McCullough's who was his idol and Bill Nicholson and he was coming in from right field. The boys were all excited with their newly acquired trophies.

It was Monday morning. John was up at 5:00 am to finish up the heavy amount of clothes that came in last week for cleaning. He didn't mind it at all; business was good. It won't be long before they start looking for their own home. Joe told him that as soon as he can find some free time, he would start teaching John how to drive. John was in no hurry, as long as he could get around with public transportation.

He was ironing clothes for about two hours when a man who he had never seen before walked into the store. He told John that he had a knife and wanted John's money. John tried to reason with the man, but he told John that he would cut him up if he didn't deliver the money. The man started swearing at him and moved the knife in his direction. John still had his hand on the heavy iron and swung it upwards, then came down on the side of the man's head. Blood splattered the walls and John's new sign. The knife flew out of the man's hand, landing on the far side of the room. The thief was getting up, trying to head for the door when John hit him in the back with the hot iron. The thief screamed, which could be heard for blocks, bolting out the door, flying up the steps, heading for a car that was waiting for him. The blood was oozing out of the thief's head, onto the steps and sidewalk. He jumped into the car, with John in pursuit. As John got to the sidewalk, he heard the screeching of the car's tires. They were gone in seconds.

A woman crossing the street heard the tires screeching and looked up to see the fast-moving car approaching her. She leaped to the side, the car missing her by a few inches. A policeman in civilian clothes going to work saw the car veering and missing the woman and decided to follow the car.

The thieves made a quick turn and headed for the hospital. The policeman noticed the bleeding thief and knew where they were heading. The thieves turned into the emergency entrance. Once in front of the door, one thief ran into the hospital. A few seconds later, a stretcher was brought out and the bleeding thief, who lost a great deal of blood, was wheeled into the emergency room. The policeman outside who witnessed it all called his precinct and asked for assistance. It wasn't long before two patrol cars came and were briefed on the situation.

The thief with the gun was looking out the window and saw the patrol cars arrive. He ran into the bathroom, hoping they weren't looking for him. The cops came in with guns drawn, looking for the thief. A man in the waiting room motioned to one of the cops that he saw a man run into the bathroom. The two cops entered the men's room and noticed feet in one of the stalls. The cops said for him to come out with hands over his head or they will fire into the stall. "I'm coming out, " cried the thief. "Don't shoot". As he came out, the gun in his hand, he fired one shot, hitting one cop, as the other cop emptied his gun into the thief, who fell backwards into the stall, dead.

John was informed by a policeman who came to his shop. Mary was there, cleaning up the blood that was all over the walls. The knife the thief had dropped was still on the floor. The officer thanked John for his help and then left. He also told John that the officer who was shot would fully recover. The rains came that night and washed away most of the blood on the steps and sidewalk.

Months went by and John read in the papers that the thief he had hit with the iron was sentenced to ten years in prison.

One day while passing the school bulletin board, Steve noticed that a CYO club was forming and needed softball players. "If interested, come down to the classroom on Friday", stated the bulletin. Steve thought about it and decided that he would go down to the classroom and find out more information.

When he entered the room on Friday, he was surprised to see all the boys and girls there. A priest came over to Steve and introduced himself as Father Joe, and asked him if he was here to sign up for the softball team. "Yes", said Steve. "Well", said Father Joe who headed up the club, "we will be getting together tomorrow and every Saturday. If you're interested, we would be happy to have you come down and try out for the team". "Great, I'll be there", declared Steve.

There were ping-pong tables in the hall on one side of the room, so Steve walked over and picked up a paddle and was looking at it when a pretty girl walked over and asked if he would like to play. Steve agreed, eyeing her pretty face. He felt awkward at first, playing a girl, but she was good at the game and almost beat him. He beat her two games in a row, but it felt as if she let him win. "My name is Barbara", she said, trying to get Steve to talk to her. "I'm Steve", he said. "It's my first time here". "I know", she said.

The record player came on, and Barbara asked him to dance. "I don't know how to dance", Steve said, "and to be honest, I never tried". "Come on", she said. "I'll show you". It was a slow dance, and Steve didn't want to say no. She showed him the two-step, and having her in his arms, he did well. They danced a few more slow dances, and then sat and talked. Whenever a fast record came on, Barbara would dance with one of her girlfriends she came with, but always asked Steve if he minded. Steve was happy he came, especially since meeting Barbara.

When it was time to go home, Barbara asked Steve if he would like to go with her and her friends to a soda shop near there. "Sure", he said. They all walked and talked on the way. Steve, telling her about the boat ride to America to escape the Germans. He walked Barbara home afterwards, and while they walked and talked, their hands touched. Barbara reached over and took Steve's hand, giving him a smile. Barbara was almost eighteen and a senior in high school. She confided to Steve her plans after high school. She would go to a college close to home for two years, and then make a decision about what she wants to do with her life. "My parents want me to go to an Ivy League college for four years. We constantly argue about this". "Well", said Steve, "your parents want the best for their little girl". "I know", said Barbara, "but that's not what I want". "It's still time for them to reconsider", said Steve. "I know", said Barb, and moved in close to give him a kiss. "Goodnight Steve", she said. "Goodnight, Barb. Maybe if you have time, you can come to the park tomorrow and watch us practice". "I'll see", she said, and went into her house. Steve had a smile on his face on the way home. He couldn't wait to get home and tell his mother about Barbara and the good time he had.

John was finding free time in the evenings, so he told Joe that anytime he wanted to take him out driving, he would have the time to go. So that evening Joe said to him, "Let's go, John. The lesson awaits you". The first two days were the toughest. John would release the clutch too fast, and it felt like they were riding a bull in a rodeo. Joe was an excellent instructor, with the patience of a saint. He kept telling John to relax and slowly release the clutch as he gives it some gas and puts the car in gear. It took a few days and finally he started to catch John. Eleanor asked Joe how John was doing, as he was taking an aspirin. He laughed as he answered her, saying it was a struggle. But John is catching on. He added that he wasn't sure what would go first, the clutch or him. A week went by, and Joe told John that he felt that he was ready to take his driving test. Joe took John for his test and he passed easily. Jhon walked into his kitchen, waving his license for Mary to see. "Great", said Mary. "Now let's go out and buy a car".

John and Mary decided to get a car. It didn't have to be a new one, but one that would run and not give him any trouble. Since John knew nothing about the workings of a car, he asked Joe, who was a part-time mechanic in Poland. They went to a few car dealers and looked at many cars, until John spotted a shiny black Ford that hit his eye. They took it for a test drive with Joe at the wheel. They went for a short distance and Joe pulled over to the curb and inspected it completely. The car, as far as Joe could see, was good for the price they were asking. He told John the car was worth the price. So John was happy and bought it. They all got into the car and John was in his glory to drive it home. He parked it out front, and all the next day he kept looking at it from his front window. When Steve saw it, the first thing he said to his Dad was, "when are you going to teach me how to drive"? "Easy, Steve", said his Dad. "Let me enjoy the car for awhile and later it will be your turn, OK"? "Yes, Dad", he said. The next evening John asked Mary if she wanted to take a ride. "In my lady", he said. They rode with the radio playing and the windows opened, since it was a hot day. The two felt like teenagers. "Do you want to stop and park", he asked Mary. "Oh John", she said laughing.

Steve was at the park early, anxious to play. Father Joe arrived a short time later and got the boys together. He started rotating the boys in different positions, looking to see where they play best. After two hours of practicing, he called it a day, thanking the boys for coming. He told the boys that the list of the first squad of players would be posted on the board by the end of the week. Steve was disappointed that Barbara didn't show up, thinking for sure that she would. He thought of calling her, but didn't want to sound pushy. He thought he would see her that Friday at the hall.

Friday came, and Steve got all dressed up, all excited about seeing Barbara again. He walked over to the bulletin board and looked for his name. He found it, listing him to play first base. He glanced at the rest of the list, looking to see if he knew the rest of the team players. He felt a soft tap on his shoulder, and a soft-spoken voice. "Hi, Steve", she said, "I missed you". "Hi, Barb", he said. "I made the team. "I knew you would", she said. "I'm sorry I couldn't go to watch you at practice. My Dad had me typing and running errands all day". That's OK", he said, feeling a lot better now. Father Joe walked in and came over to Steve. He asked Steve to be the captain of the team. He noticed that boys looked up to Steve. "Fine with me, Father", he said. He told Steve that they would be getting measured for their uniforms after practice tomorrow. "Great", said Steve. "I can't wait to tell the guys".

Chapter IX

Steve was starting to feel bad that he wasn't driving, as were most of the boys his age. His Dad wasn't experienced enough himself to start teaching Steve to drive. His friends who were driving would usually take Barbara and him places, but he felt bad about that because at times he felt like going other places than where they were going, but had to tag along with them. He was getting desperate now, and went to see Uncle Joe, and explained the situation to him. He told him his father was always too busy to teach him, laying it on thick. Joe, who loved Steve like his own, told him that he would teach him if he got his Dad's permission. "Great", he said, and hurried down to his Dad's store to tell him. Steve proceeded to tell his Dad about asking Joe to teach him to drive and hoped it was OK with him that he did ask. John felt bad that he couldn't teach his son to drive. "I don't mind", he said, "but you be careful with the car". "I sure will, Dad", he said and gave his Dad a hug. With a tear in his eye, he told Steve, "Now go scat, Tiger". Steve took the stairs two at a time. Joe opened the door as he heard Steve run up the steps. "My Dad said OK, Uncle Joe". "Fine", said Joe. "How about starting your first lesson this Saturday afternoon"? "Great", said Steve, showing that he was ecstatic and couldn't wait to tell Barbara.

Their first softball game was played on Sunday morning, and Barbara came with her younger sister, Donna, a cute brunette who was 15. She loved sports and baseball was her favorite. She went with her father to watch the Chicago Cubs many times at Wrigley Field, and could name most of the players on the team.

Donny came to the park with his parents, and when Steve saw them come in, he waved and called out for them to come over where he was so he could introduce Barbara and her sister, Donna, to them. Father Joe stopped over by them, and Steve introduced his family to him. "You have a very nice son in Steve", he said. They thanked him, and Father Joe turned to Donny and said, "I haven't seen you down at the hall on Fridays. You are more than welcome to come down". "Thank you", said Donny. "Maybe I'll stop over there this Friday". "Good", Father Joe said, as he turned to walk out to the field.

Donna looked over at Donny and said, "I hear you like the Cubs". Donny said yes, and the two of them talked so much that they lost track of the game they came to watch. When Steve came over to them, Donny asked him what the score was. "I'm glad you two came to watch our game", he said with a smile on his face. Embarrassed with a red face, Donny looked at Donna who was giggling at him and said, "I think we better watch the rest of the game". Steve's team had an easy win, 8 to 2. After the game, Steve asked Donny if he wanted to walk home with Barbara and Donna. "Sure", he said as he rushed over to tell his parents.

Mary looked over at John and said, "It looks like our boys are growing up and don't need us anymore". "That's the painful thing about kids growing up", he said. "They're no longer babies and we have to accept the fact that they will soon leave the nest". "Well, I sure don't have to like that fact", she said.

Steve told Barbara about his Uncle Joe teaching him how to drive. "Soon we'll be going to places we want to go', he said, "instead of tagging along with the others". "Can Donny and I go with you guys", asked Donna. "I guess so", said Steve, glancing over for Barbara's approval to what he just told Donna. "Sure they can. We would enjoy having you guys double with us", smiling as she said it. Steve was doing well with his driving lessons, much better than his father did. After two weeks of lessons, Steve was driving well enough to take his driving test. He used his Dad's car with Joe coming along for support. He passed easily and got his drivers license. He drove home, feeling great. He couldn't wait to call Barbara and tell her the good news. He was planning on taking her for a ride later on, just the two of them. Oh, how great life is!

Barbara's parents, Frank and Rose Young, liked Steve, but felt Barbara could do better. They wanted the best for her, wanted her to go to an Ivy League College for four years, and then go to law school for three years. Barbara was planning to go to a junior college near home, so that she could continue seeing Steve. Frank, a well-to-do attorney in town, had a great practice. Barbara had been helping him on weekends and sometimes after school, doing clerical functions for him, but mostly typing. She could type 60 words a minute and is very accurate. She is in her second year of steno, which helps her considerably. Her Dad can picture her as a fine lawyer. He would like to see her break off her relationship with Steve, but wouldn't want to say too much to hurt his little girl. Frank spoke to Steve and told him how he felt about Barbara going to college and her bright future. Steve told Barbara about his talk with her Dad. Maybe she should consider her father's wishes. "He's only looking out for your future", Steve told her. Barbara went into a rage when she saw her father. She stopped talking to him, even stopped going to the office to help him. Her Mom tried to stay out of it; there was no way was she going to take sides.

Friday evening came, and Steve asked Donny if he wanted to ride to the hall. "OK", said Donny, feeling better to go with Steve, since he didn't know anyone there. They were the first ones there, and they headed for the ping-pong tables. Here Donny played well, but was no match for Steve who beat him three straight games. "Have you had enough, little brother"? "No", said Donny. "One more game". The crowd gathered to watch them play.

Father Joe walked over to them. "Hi, guys", he said. "I'm glad you could come, Donny". "Well, I'm not sure if I am, Father", said Donny. "My brother beat me three straight games, and I thought I was good at this game". "He beat me, too", said Father Joe. "But I was just lucky that game", said Steve and laughed. Barbara walked in with her sister, Donna, and headed for the brothers. "Can I play the winner", asked Donna? "Sure", said Steve, and then let Donny beat him so he could be with Barbara. The music came on, and Steve asked Barbara to dance. Donna looked at Donny and said, "Do you want to dance"? "No"', said Donny. "I would rather beat you at ping-pong". "Oh yea", said Donna. "Let's play, big boy". Donny beat her, but it was close enough of a score to make Donny think that maybe she let him win. When then left the hall, they all walked to the soda shop, both couples holding hands as they walked.

Donny got a job as a soda jerk at the shop they go to every Friday after CTO. He worked after school for a few hours, and full days on weekends. It was getting rough on him on weekends, because he missed not seeing Donna. The place he worked at wasn't far from where Donna lived, so she would stop in and see him a few times a week. The owner didn't complain to him because he saw that it never interfered with his work. He was a hard worker, and a fast learner. And he sure didn't want to lose Donny. He got Fridays off so he could go to the hall. When the crowd came afterwards, Donny would jump right in to take the orders and stay afterwards to clean up. Donna would stay and help him clean up, and then he would walk her home. Sunday was always a slow day and he only worked a half-day.

When the boys went to the hall one Friday, they were surprised to see the Middleweight Champion of the World standing with Father Joe. When most of the boys got there, Father Joe introduced the boys to the champ, and said that he was getting together a boxing team to represent their club. If anyone was interested, sign the paper on the table. "One final thing", he said. "The champ will be here for a couple of weeks to help train anyone. Steve told Donny that he should sign up, and to impress Donna, he signed. Training would take place every day after school at a local park near the school. Donna told Donny that she would fill in for him at the soda shop so he could train. Donny didn't enjoy running or exercising, but getting into the ring he enjoyed. He liked boxing other boys, even heavier guys than him. He was ready when Father Joe said that their first boxing match was coming up in a week. The few boys who made the team, including Donny, were given green satin shorts and white tee shirts with the CYO logo.

The fighting match was scheduled at a park near them, and Steve said he would drive him there. When they got there, they were sent to the gym and given a locker to get ready. The first fight was on, and it was fought to a draw. In the second fight, the boy on his team lost; he got a bloody nose and the referee stopped the fight. In the third fight, the boy on his team lost due to a cut lip, and the referee stopped the fight. Donny was told to get ready to enter the ring. Father Joe met him as he left the locker room, and wished him good luck. As he came into the ring, he glanced over and looked at all the people who came to watch the fights. He didn't recognize anyone.

Chapter X

Steve told him to sit down in the chair that was in the corner. Donny looked over at the boy in the other corner, who was smiling at him. A little older than him, he thought, and he weighted more than Donny did. Donny smiled back at him. The announcer started to speak. "Now in the red corner, weighing in at one hundred forty pounds and comes from Grapeville, Richard Peterson". A loud roar came from the crowd. "And in the white corner, weighing in at one hundred thirty-five pounds, representing the CYO Club North, Donny Kalomowski". Donny was waiting for the roar of the crowd, but only got some handclaps. The referee got the boys in the center of the ring, and gave them some final instructions about not hitting below the belt and to listen to him. He wished them both good luck and they touched gloves. They were told to wait for the bell to ring.

The bell rang, and Donny went to the center of the ring to meet his opponent, who was already there. Donny jabbed and moved around the ring. The other boy jabbed back and threw his right hand, hitting Donny on the side of the head. The crowd roared, expecting Donny to be dazed, but Donny just backed up and smiled at the boy, telling him he wasn't hurt. Again the boy rushed him, and again Donny backed up. Steve was yelling at him now, "Throw your right, throw your right". Donny kept jabbing. "OK", said Steve, "now stop dancing around. The bell rang, ending round one.

Donny walked to his corner and sat down. "What's the matter, Donny", asked Steve. "Why", said Donny? "He isn't hurting me; I know what I'm doing. "OK", Steve said, "but you two look like your dancing instead of boxing". The bell rang and Donny was out first, thinking of what Steve had said. "OK", he thought, "let's go to work". He jabbed once, twice, and his opponent lowered his arms for a brief second. Donny heard Steve yell, "Now, Donny". Donny then threw his right with full force, landing the punch right into the boy's nose. He heard the crushing blow and saw crimson red spurt from the boy's nose. He backed up as the boy went to his knees. The referee was there in a second, waving Donny to his corner. The boy was bleeding badly, and the referee waved the fight over, helping the boy to his corner. Steve was yelling now. "Great fight, Donny", but Donny wasn't too happy. He felt badly for the boy who now had a towel, holding it to his nose to stop the bleeding.

Father Joe made his way to Donny, and told him "Good fight. We needed that win to guarantee a tie, with two more fights to go". Donny went to the locker where he saw Donna standing outside. She went to him and gave him a hug. "Are you OK", she asked. "Sure", he said, "but I feel bad about the other guy I hurt". Steve heard him and said, "He's OK, Donny. He's in the shower right now, and you'll see him when he comes out". Donny told Steve that he would like to see the last two fights. "Sure", said Steve. "Now go take your shower". "I'll wait for you here", said Donna. "OK", he said, and went inside. The boy he beat came up to him all cleaned up from his shower and went to shake Donny's hand. "Good fight", he said. "Yea", said Donny.

After the hot shower, he felt like a new person. He met Donna, who waited for him, and whistled at him. "I feel better", he said. "Now let's go see how we do in the last two fights". The next fight went to the other team, and the last fight was ready to start. Donny was up and down in his chair, trying to rally his teammate on. It wasn't to be, because the boy was cut on the eyebrow, and the fight was stopped. "Nuts", said Donny. Father Joe, who was near and heard his remark, said, "We got a tie, which is good for our first match". "I guess", said Donny. When they got to the car, Steve said, "How about we go to the soda shop. The treat's on me". "Wow", said Donny. "That's the first time I ever heard you say that". "Baloney", said Steve. "I've supported you for years; how easy we forget". "Take it easy now, boys", said Barbara.

Barbara was on her way to the bank, which was a five-minute walk from her house. She wanted to cash her weekly check that she received from her father. She felt that she really earned her money this week. Since her argument with her Dad, she had not talked to him. That hurt her, but she wouldn't give in. she went and did her work and only spoke to him when it was necessary. He wasn't happy about it, either, but would not give in. It was lunchtime, and she wanted to open a savings account. She already had a checking account with a few dollars left in it. She was not one to hold onto money. She was lucky to have a few dollars left over each month. Opening a savings account may help her save some money each month.

The bank looked crowded as she walked in. She got in line and prepared to wait it out. She glanced around, looking at the customers in the bank. She noticed three men wearing Chicago Cubs baseball hats, and all three had dark sunglasses on. That was peculiar, because it was cloudy and getting dark out, like a storm was brewing. She dismissed them and continued her glance to others at the counter. She spotted another man with a Cubs hat and dark glasses. Her peripheral vision caught another baseball hat at the center table. She got scared then, realizing what was going to happen. Just then, the men announced that the bank was being robbed. They were all holding guns and taking positions by the front clerks. The guard near the front door, a retired policeman and near retirement age, went to remove his gun from his holster, but never succeeded in doing it because the thief at the middle table was watching him and shot him as he went for his gun. The guard went down on his knees, looking surprised, never seeing the thief who shot him. The thief at the table with a smoking gun in his hand said, "I told you all to behave. So let me assure you, we mean business. Everyone sit down where you are". Barbara sat down and started to feel sick to her stomach. "He didn't have to shoot that poor guard", she thought.

Chapter XI

One brave woman teller saw that she had a chance to hit the silent alarm, and did without being seen. This informed the police of a robbery in progress. One thief kept his eyes peeled behind the curtain, watching for any activity outside in the streets. Now and then a customer would walk in and was escorted to the center of the room and told to sit down with the rest of the customers. Barbara glanced over at the bleeding guard, who isn't moving now. She felt like crying, but was too scared to do so. The woman in front of Barbara was crying, and asked the thief if she could go to the bathroom. "No", he cried out, "and stop your crying". As he waved his gun at her, the woman started to sob and shake. Barbara reached over and put her arm around the woman, trying to console her. Another thief, seeing this, came over to them and asked what the trouble was. "She has to go to the bathroom, like the rest of us", said Barbara. "No way", he said. "Hold it a little longer and we will be out of here soon. Nobody leaves this area, is that understood?" he said. "OK", said the woman, still crying and shaking.

The thief went to the front window, pulled back the shades and turned white. The street was full of police. "Cops", he cried out. "The place is crawling with them". The two thieves behind the cages gathering the money stopped what they were doing and jumped over the ledge to join the others to look at the police. "What do we do now", asked one of the robbers. The leader of the group, who had a goatee, said, "Get all those people and line them up by the window. Let's show those cops what we have here". They got Barbara and the rest of the customers and put them all in front of the window. They pulled back the curtains and showed the police all the hostages they had. They quickly closed the drapes and told the people to go back to where they were sitting. Goatee figured he now had the upper hand, and the police would think twice before rushing them in the bank.

The police set up a loudspeaker and told the robbers to come out with their hands up and no one would get hurt. The leader laughed when he heard that and said, "I guess they don't know about him", pointing to the guard who looked dead to him. The leader went to the front door and opened it a crack. He yelled out, "We have twelve hostages in the bank and will kill them if one shot is fired by the police.

John and Mary were listening to the news like they usually did when they heard of the bank robbery so close to home. No hostage names were given, so they had no idea that Barbara was one of them. Steve called Barbara to see what they were going to do that evening, and was told that she wasn't home yet. Her parents began to worry when hours passed and she didn't come home. They called Steve and asked if he had any idea where she could have gone. Steve mentioned that she told him that she planned to go to the bank at lunchtime, but that was all. At that point, Frank cried out, "Oh my God, she may be one of the hostages at the bank".

They told him about the robbery, and he slammed down the phone and headed for the bank. When he got there, Frank and Rose just arrived. "Is she in the bank", asked Steve. The police have no names yet. The police placed sharpshooters across the street from the bank, but with the drapes drawn, they couldn't see anyone in the bank. The loudspeaker blurted out again, "Please release the hostages". A voice yelled back from the door, "No way, and pull those snipers off the roofs or we will give you a dead hostage". "You have two minutes", the loudspeaker said.

Just then the sniper said he had a clear shot at one of the robbers. The drapes moved a little, exposing a man with a gun. A voice came back to the sniper, "Take him out if you get a clear shot". A shot rang out, a window in the bank broke. Inside the bank, Goatee saw one of his men hit in the chest and lay dead, close to where the hostages sat. Screams were heard from the hostages as they looked at the dead thief. Goatee, now fuming, went to the hostages and told the woman who asked to go to the bathroom to get up. She followed him to the front door, which opened, and told her to walk to the police. "Do not run", he said. The woman squeezed through the door, looked back at Barbara and smiled. She saw her freedom 25 yards away, and started to run. Goatee raised his pistol and fired, hitting her in the back. She managed to take a few more steps, then collapsed. The crowd gathered across the street behind the police barricade gasped. Goatee opened the door a little and yelled out, "Get rid of those snipers, or two more hostages will follow". He then slammed the door shut.

Goatee went over to make sure the drapes were closed, and as he did, he passed by Barbara and said, "She doesn't have to go to the bathroom now, does she"? He was smiling as he continued to check the drapes. Barbara whispered as she followed him with her eyes,

"You dirty butcher".

The police brought over a barricade on wheels, used to rescue fallen comrades. A few officers got behind the barricade, which was made of thick wood that would stop any bullets coming its way. The officers rolled it towards the woman who was shot. When they got there, they reached over and pulled her behind the barricade. They rolled them to a safe area. An ambulance was waiting and took her to a hospital. The officers who attended to her said that she was alive, but lost a lot of blood. At the hospital she was taken directly to the operating room and given a blood transfusion. When her vital signs were good, a team of doctors operated on her to remove the bullet lodged in her back.

Goatee once again opened the front door and insisted that a bus filled with gas be brought to the front entrance of the bank. He ordered that all the seats be taken out except for the driver's seat, and two seats in front. "No police in the bus", he cried out, "or hostages will die. He slammed the door shut.

Chapter XII

Frank, Rose and Steve were behind the police barricades, worried sick. "Maybe they will release the hostages when the bus arrives", said Frank. "I sure hope so', said Steve. Father Joe arrived on the scene, after hearing about the robbery. He didn't know that Barbara was a hostage until he saw Steve standing there. "I'm sorry", he said, trying his best to console them. The police got the bus there in less than a half-hour. Goatee saw it come and went to the door. He called out, "Start up the bussand let it run". The police did as they were told and started the bus. After a half-hour, the bus stalled out. "Kick it over again", he cried out. The bus wouldn't start up. Goatee opened the door again and yelled out, "Let's try it again, boys, but this time bring a bus filled with gas, and no water in it. No more tricks. You are wearing down my patience". A two truck came and removed the first bus.

Steve yelled over to the police to stop playing games with the hostages' lives and give them a bus so that they will free the hostages. Goatee overheard Steve's remark and said; "Now that's a smart man". The commander in charge would not look in Steve's direction, feeling embarrassed for the first bus goof.

Goatee and his companions hadn't eaten since early morning, and complained to Goatee about getting some food brought in. Goatee went to the door, opened it a crack, and yelled out that they want food delivered to the front door. "I want hot dogs, hamburgers, salads and soda and beer". The commander got on the speaker and said food would be delivered only after they gave out the names of all the hostages. Goatee thought about it for a moment and said it wouldn't hurt to give them the names. He ordered a clerk hostage to get a clipboard and go around and write everyone's names. After everyone put their names on the paper, Goatee took the clipboard, went to the front door, and tossed it out as far as he could.

Steve, seeing the clipboard hit the pavement, jumped over the barricade and raced for the clipboard. He did this so fast that no one could stop him, or even call out for him to stop. He got to the clipboard in seconds, picked it up, and as he was heading back to the barricade, glanced at the names to find Barbara on the list. The commander was waiting for him, and as he came over the barricade, he grabbed the clipboard from his hands, screaming at him. "That was a stupid stunt, kid', he cried out. "If you give me any more trouble, I will put handcuffs on you and put you in the van. Do I make myself clear", he roared. "Yes, sir", Steve replied, but kept looking at the ground. The reporters gathered around the Commander as he read the names of the hostages. Once the reporters got the list, they all left, heading for phones.

Food arrived and was wheeled out to the front door of the bank. Goatee had two of his men bring in the food and had them set it up on the center table. He told the hostages to get up and help themselves to the food, making sure the food wasn't laced with any drugs to make them sick. Barbara asked Goatee if she could use the bathroom, which was located near the front door. "OK", he told her, "but don't be stupid and try to escape. Remember that I have all these hostages and will kill them if you try anything foolish". When she came out, she thanked him and then went to the table with the food on it. Seeing that no one got sick and everyone at goatee and his men started to eat.

After Goatee and his men finished eating and having a few beers, he went to the front window, drew back the drapes a little, and saw a new bus out in front. The doors were opened and he could see the steering wheel and the front seat all intact. There were seats that were taken out of the bus, piled alongside it. So far, so good. They expect him to tell them to start up the bus, he thought, but he won't. Why waste the gas? They wouldn't be stupid enough to try the water routine again.

The agency that hires guards for the bank called the police when they heard about the robbery. They told the police about the guard at the bank, and wanted to know if he was a hostage. The Commander got on the loudspeaker and asked about the guard and if he was a hostage. Goatee went to the door, opened it a little, and cried out that the guard was in the bank but couldn't talk to anyone. He couldn't tell the police the guard was dead or all the talks would come to an end. He couldn't risk it. "He's tied up in the back', he yelled out. "Untie him and bring him to the window, " yelled the Commander, sensing that something was wrong. "Can't do", yelled Goatee. "The talks are over", cried out the Commander. Goatee started to panic. "Drag the guard over here by the window", he yelled out to his two men. "We have to make it look like he's alive, or this job is over". They dragged the guard to the window and tried to hold him up while Goatee opened the drapes a little. "Hold him while I go to the door. Here's you guard", he cried out. But it backfired on him. The two men couldn't hold him up, and he just slumped over. The snipers across the street called out that they had a good contact with the robbers. Goatee rushed over to close the door when he saw his plan had fizzled out.

Goatee went to the front door, opened it, and called out to the police, "The stupid old man went for his gun, and my man had to shoot. You can tell his family that he was a hero to the end". He was smiling now, figuring that he still had the upper hand holding all the hostages. "That's it", cried the Commander. "I'm bringing in the SWAT team'. The police stopped negotiating with the robbers, which had Goatee in an uproar now. The bus was removed from the front of the bank. Goatee and his men were watching as the bus was removed. Goatee started thinking that it was a mistake telling them about the dead guard, but it wasn't over. He still had the hostages, he thought, so he went to the door, opened it, and yelled to the police to bring back the bus or a hostage would die. There was no response from the police. A minute passed, and two vans arrived right in front where the empty bus once was parked.

Chapter XIII

"Oh, no", cried Goatee, seeing the two vans arrive. "It's the SWAT team". The loudspeaker came on and everyone listened. "This is Commander Foster", he cried out. "You have no chance of escape. You killed a guard and shot a defenseless woman. My advice to you is to come out with your hands over your heads. We will hold our fire while you do so; otherwise, we will have to come in and take you by force".

Barbara glanced over to the front door and noticed it ajar from Goatee last using it. She thought maybe she could get there without being seen, and to safety. The backs of the robbers were to her, so she quickly took off her shoes, sprang to her feet, and was on the way to the door. She got to the door unnoticed by Goatee and his men. She opened the door and made a fast dash for the safety of the police. Goatee never saw her until she was at the door, and it was too late to stop her. Barbara just made it to safety. Two SWAT team officers got to her in a second, and escorted her to a van. Barbara was allowed to rest for a while, and then the SWAT team commander started to question her. She broke down and cried when asked about the killing of the guard and shooting of the woman. "The butcher with the goatee shot her for no reason. She couldn't hurt him", she cried. "She only wanted to use the bathroom. He told me that she won't have to use the bathroom anymore after he shot her".

Steve was standing next to Barbara, holding her hand, and asked the SWAT commander if he could stop the questioning. He didn't want Barbara getting upset. "Yes", he said, "we will need her later on, after we get those men out of the bank". Goatee was now upset, letting Barbara escape, and he knew that the SWAT team would soon break in and kill them. "We don't have a chance", cried one of the robbers, "not with the SWAT team and the weapon power they have". "OK", said Goatee, knowing the end was near. He went to the door and called out that they were releasing the hostages, and then will come out. "Hold your fire", he cried out. He got the hostages up and let them out the door. Goatee and his men followed with hands raised. A few SWAT officers rushed to meet them and got them on the ground, searching them for weapons and then handcuffing them and putting them in the meat wagon for a trip to jail. The SWAT team entered the bank and carried out the dead old guard. "What a shame", said one officer.

The doorbell rang while the family was having breakfast. Frank got up to answer the door, and found her standing there, a young pretty blonde woman who was in her late 20's. "Hello", he said, "May I help you"? "I'm a reporter for the Chicago Herald", she said. I'd like to speak to Barbara if I could, please. "Come in", said Frank, "While I go and ask her. He went to his daughter and told her a reporter was in the hallway and would like to speak with her. "Oh, OK", said Barbara. "I might as well get it over with". Frank went to the woman and invited her in. She showed frank her identification card with her picture on it. "My name is Ann Cole", she said, reaching out her hand to his. He took her into the kitchen and introduced Barbara and his wife to her. "What a pretty, warm kitchen this is", she said. "Why not stay right here and talk". "Fine", said Barbara, and sat down. Frank sat down next to her and Ann opposite them. Rose was at the stove and said, "I'll make us a fresh pot of coffee to go with the Bobka I bought at the bakery yesterday". "Great", said Ann and Rose started to set the table. Ann started by asking Barbara's full name, age and other personal questions. Then she asked about the bank. "What time did you get there", she asked? "Around 9:30", she said. "I noticed how crowded the bank was and got in line for the long wait. I glanced around at the people in the bank, and then noticed these three men, all wearing the same baseball hats and dark glasses. It was odd, I thought, because the sun wasn't out yet. Two of the men were at the teller's cage; the other was at the table, looking all around. All of a sudden the two men at the tellers cage took out guns, and started yelling about a holdup. I glanced over at the man at the table, and he was taking out a gun and aimed it at the front door. My eyes went to the front door. I saw the older guard who was reaching for his gun, and just as he was taking it out of his holster, the next thing I heard was this loud bang and the guard grabbed his chest, dropping his gun to the floor. I wanted to scream, but couldn't". The guard took a step backward and another shot rang out and the guard slowly fell to the floor, blood oozing on the floor". Ann, seeing Barbara start to shake, stopped her questioning and said, "Why not stop now and have some of that delicious Bobka and coffee". Frank put his arm around Barbara and said, "Do you want to call it a day? Are you OK"? "I'm OK, Dad, I just need a few minutes, and I'll be fine".

Rose got up and went to the counter and got the Bobka and brought it over to the table. The coffee was done and smelled great. Frank started pouring the coffee, while Rose was cutting everyone a piece of cake. Ann looked at Rose and asked, "You have another daughter, right"? "Yes", said Rose. "She left for school already. Her name is Donna". Ann was a real professional, staying away from talk of the bank robbery and talking about the girls growing up. When they finished their coffee and Bobka, Rose cleared off the table and then went back to sit down. After everyone was seated, Ann then proceeded to ask Barbara to continue if she felt up to it. Ann finished the interview as fast as she could. She thanked Barbara and Frank. She told Rose the Bobka was the best she had eaten and asked Rose for the directions to the bakery so she could stop there. She told Barbara that she might have to go to court when the robbers' trial came up. "She is aware of that", said Frank. Ann made a few steps toward the door, and Frank was there, opening the door for her. "Thank you again", she said as she left. "That wasn't so bad", said Barbara to her Dad. "It may be worse when you get on the stand and the prosecutor asks the questions". "I'm not afraid of that", said Barbara. "Wait for me, Daddy, and I'll come down to the office with you". They were close again. Even Steve and her father were friends now, after her episode at the bank. He saw how much Steve cared for his little girl and knew he would take care of her. Something good came out of something bad.

Some of Steve's friends had been receiving their greetings from Uncle Sam. When he went to the hall on Friday, he mentioned to Barbara that he couldn't see enlisting in the service for four years. He will wait for the draft board to send him his notice and go from there. Donny said that as soon as he turns 18, he would enlist in the Navy. "Good for you", said Steve. "How about we take a ride to Diamond Lake this Sunday and go eat. I hear they have the best ribs around", Steve said. "I think that's a great idea", said Barbara. "Donny and Donna can come with us", she said. "OK, that's settled". Donna and Donny were on the ping-pong tables. Donny was getting good at the game and could beat Steve once and awhile now. Father Joe walked in and headed straight for Donny. "Hi, Donny", he said. "We just got word that the next boxing tournament is in two weeks.

Do you think you will be ready for it"? "Sure", said Donny. "I'm ready now", he said with a big grin on his face. "I sure hope so", said Father Joe, "because I hear that the park has some tough boxers on their team". "I'll be ready", he said. Father Joe walked over to Steve and Barbara to tell Steve the news. Some of the girls were asking Barbara about the bank robbery, and Father Joe saw how unpleasant she looked answering. Father Joe got all the kids together and started out by telling them about the upcoming boxing tournament, and then mentioned that Barbara had been through a lot. "Let's not ask her anymore about the bank robbery". Everyone started to applaud. Barbara came up to Father Joe and whispered, "Thank you".

On December 7, the family was in the kitchen having breakfast, when a neighbor came to the door and cried out, "Put your radio on. Pearl Harbor was just attacked by the Japanese. The President declared war on them for their sneaky attack. "Oh my God", said Mary, fearing for her two boys. John and boys had their ears glued to the radio. "We are at war on both fronts", said John. "I want to enlist in the Marines", cried Donny. "Hold on, Donny", said John. You won't be 18 for another month. Let's wait until then". "OK Dad", he said. Donny looked over at Steve and said, "How about you, Steve? I'll be drafted soon enough. With the two of us there, the Germans or the Japs won't stand a chance". "Hey, how about we go see the girls", Steve said, trying to get away from the war talk. When the boys got there, the girls were sitting on the front porch.

"Did you hear the radio", asked Donny. "Yes", said Barbara. "We're at war". "Those dirty Japs bombed us", cried Donny. "We will give them a beating they will never forget".

Chapter XIV

With all the news about the war and Barbara's court date, the four of them wanted to get away for the day. So they took a ride to Diamond Lake, a restaurant that advertises the best ribs in the state. It was a good hour's trip, but proved to be a good choice. The ribs, which they all ordered, were the best they had ever had. But Barbara said, "The next time we come here we should all bring a roll of paper towels with us". They all laughed and agreed.

Barbara's day in court came, and her Dad and his partner, Bill, came along so the other lawyers would not take advantage of her. She always thought it was good to have a lawyer in the family. As Barbara walked into the courtroom, she spotted Goatee and his two accomplices. Goatee was in a gray suit and clean, almost good looking. He smiled at her when their eyes met, bringing back that horrible day at the bank. She turned her eyes away from him. The day seemed to drag by, and finally the time came when Barbara was called to the stand. She told her story from the time she entered the bank and got nervous. When she was asked if she saw the man herein the courtroom who shot the guard at the bank, she said she did and pointed to Goatee. She was then asked if the man who shot the woman was in the courtroom. She got up from the stand and said, "Yes". She told the court that the man who shot the woman was the man wearing the gray suit today and that he also shaved off his goatee. Barbara also said that he told her that the woman would not have to go to the bathroom anymore. It didn't take the jury long to find all three guilty. Goatee got the electric chair, and the other two men got life sentences.

Steve's softball team was doing well. They were in first place and were in the playoffs, which were to start in a week. Father Joe was proud of his team, and told them so. Donny started preparing for his next fight by running two miles a day and lifting weights. He would do one hundred pushups and one hundred sit-ups before dinner. He felt as ready as he would ever be. Donna loved to run, and she would go running with him. Donny also loved tennis and took Donna to the courts to teach her how to play. She was a born athlete. More so than Barbara. Barbara loved to read books more than exercise.

Steve drove Donny and the two girls to the park so they could watch his team play in the playoffs. Father Joe was already there, getting the boys together for his pep talk when Steve arrived. The girls' parents came because Barbara asked them to, and found a seat near Mary and John. It was a beautiful sunny and warm day, a good day for a softball game, and the stands were getting full. Father Joe read off the lineup to the boys, and told them to take the field and get ready for the start of the game. "Play ball", cried out the umpire, and the game started. It was a tight game until the seventh inning when the opposing team scored a few runs and was winning 3 to 1. In the bottom of the eighth, Steve's team came up to bat, and he was the first to bat. On the first pitch, he drove a line drive past the pitcher who touched the ball, and it rolled to short center for a base hit. He heard Donny yell out, "That a boy, Steve". The next batter hit the ball deep to center field, which was caught, but gave Steve time to tag up and go to second base. The next batter hit the ball over the third baseman's head, and Steve rounded third base, but stopped in his tracks when the ball sailed over his head right to the catcher's glove. He would easily have been tagged out. Steve was now on third base with another player on second. The next boy up was a boy who was in a slump. So Father Joe put in a pinch-batter for him. The other team talked it over and went to walk him, loading up the bases, hoping for a double play, since the pitcher was coming up to bat. Father Joe decided to let the pitcher bat, since he was a fair hitter. He let the first two pitches go by. The next pitch was right over the plate, and he laid into it, hitting the ball between left and center field, scoring three runs and giving the batter a triple. The people in the stands went wild. Donny was jumping up and down and hugging Donna and then Barbara. The score was now 4 to 3 in their favor. The next batter hit the ball into right field, which was caught, but the pitcher on third base tagged up and easily scored, making the score 5 to 3. The other team scored one run in the ninth inning, but lost the game 5 to 4. Both teams shook hands after the game, a show of good sportsmanship. After the game, they all, including the parents, went to the soda shop near the park.

The team celebrated their win, and Father Joe was in his glory. Now the team was in the finals, and the #1 team would be decided on Sunday. They practiced every evening and felt good about themselves.

On Sunday father Joe got to the field early, told his team to do the same. Steve drove Donny, Barbara and Donna to the field, and the seats were getting full early. The other team took to the field first and started practicing, while Father Joe and his team looked on. "We have to beat them", said Steve. Steve's parents arrived with Barbara's parents, getting friendly since meeting them. Steve's team came up first and came up without a hit. The game remained scoreless for six innings, until the other team scored three runs in the seventh inning. Steve's team came back with one run in the eighth inning when the catcher hit a home run. The score remained 3 to 1. In the final inning, Steve's team started out by getting two hits and then, with two outs, Steve came up. He thought to himself, "I've got to get a hit", and hit the ball solid out to right field. Everyone stood up to watch the ball sail out deep, but the right fielder ran back and snatched the ball. The game was over. Steve went down on his knees, feeling bad. But Father Joe was at his side in a second, complimenting him and the team. "You guys played great", he said. The team was given second place trophies. The parents wanted to take the boys and girls to the soda shop, but Steve said no, he just wasn't up to it. Everyone understood, so they went home.

Chapter XV

Mary and John had no word about what is happening in Poland. She wondered what happened to her sister, Tes, and her brother-in-law, Kaz. He was a reporter for the paper near their town. She tried to get in touch with them through letters, but none were ever answered. Oh, how she would like to see them again. They were very close growing up, and after they got married, they tried to live near each other. Everyone she spoke to gave her the same answer. There is no word from Poland; it's as if Poland never existed. Besides her worries about her sister, and now had the worry of Steve and Donny going into the service. She hated to look at the mail anymore, waiting for the War Department to take away her two boys. "When will it end? Why can't we have peace", she thought.

Donny was training hard for his upcoming boxing match in a few more days. He liked to box and wanted to win this fight for Father Joe, who was being transferred to a New York church as pastor. Father Joe looked at it as a nice promotion. He would also be in charge of their school football team. Everyone was happy for Father Joe, but they knew that they would miss him.

The day came for Donny's boxing match, and Steve told him that he would drive him to the park, which was a few miles from them. The park was very modern. They had a boxing ring setup in the middle of the basketball court. They set up stands on both sides of the ring for easy viewing. The locker rooms were big, with huge lockers, showers and a workout room next to the showers. Very impressive! You could hear the announcer call for the first fight to begin. Donny's bout was second, and when the National Anthem was played, Steve told Donny to get dressed. "Right", said Donny, and he proceeded to put on his green boxer trunks. There was a knock on the door, and Steve answered it. Donny was told to go to the ring. The first fight was over, and his teammate was knocked out in the first round. "Oh my", said Donny, getting anxious to get going.

Donny walked into the gym, which was crowded. He was the first through the ring ropes, followed by Steve. He sat himself down in a chair that was in his corner and looked over at his opponent, who was smiling at him. He looked much heavier than Donny did, and he had a better build. But that doesn't mean too much, thought Donny. The referee got the boys together and told them he wanted a good clean fight, and then told them to go back to their corners and wait for the bell. The bell sounded, and Donny went right after the boy. He jabbed his opponent a few times, and then threw his right hand flush on the boy's jaw. The boy went down on one knee, and the referee waved to Donny to go to his corner, which he did. He could see Steve all excited. He was told by Steve to go finish him off. They were told by the referee to continue fighting. The boy was given a nine count, even though he jumped right back up. The boy smiled at Donny, letting him know that he wasn't hurt. Donny went back to jabbing his opponent, and then it happened. He dropped his arms down for a second and the other boy threw his right hand in desperation and caught Donny on the side of his face. Donny landed on his backside, stunned, but not hurt. The referee was about to start his count, but the bell sounded and Donny jumped up and went to his corner. "Are you OK", cried Steve as Donny sat down. "I'm OK", said Donny. "It was just a lucky punch that didn't hurt me, just surprised me", he said. "OK, now keep up your jabbing and throw the right hand and finish him off". "Right', Donny said. The bell rang both boys ran out to meet each other in combat. Donny jabbed a few times and then threw the right, catching the boy on the top of the head, stunning him. The boy waited for Donny to come and finish him off, but Donny paused and backed up, giving the boy a chance to recover. Steve was screaming now, "Finish him off; you've got him where you want him". His opponent rushed Donny, pushing and butting him so hard that he opened a cut over Donny's eyebrow. The blood poured out of the gash, and the referee took one look at the cut and called off the fight, disqualifying him for intentional butting. Steve rushed out to Donny with a towel, trying to stop the blood. After Donny was declared the winner, his opponent came to his corner and apologized to him. They touched gloves, and he was forgiven. Donny's victory was the only bout that Father Joe's team won.

A doctor came to Donny when he was in the locker room and checked his vision, putting a bandage on the cut to stop the bleeding. The doctor told Steve to get Donny to the hospital to have the cut stitched up. Donny got dressed, and when they left the locker room, Barbara and Donna were there to meet them. Donna gave Donny a hug, and asked him how he was. He said he felt OK. The four of them went to the hospital, which was close by, and Donny got twelve stitches to close the wound. He was told to come back in six days to have the stitches removed. "Fine", Donny said, and they left.

They left the hospital and headed for the car, with Barbara asking where they were going. "I need a hot shower", exclaimed Donny. "You sure do", laughed Steve. They dropped Donny home and said they would wait for him, then head out to the soda shop. When Donny walked into the front door of their apartment, he was greeted by his mother. When she saw his bandaged eye, she cried out, "Oh my God, Donny". "I received a few stitches, Mom". He said. "The guy I fought butted me, so they disqualified him and made me the winner. Steve and the girls are waiting for me while I take a hot shower", he said.

The hot shower felt great. He got dressed and joined Steve and the girls. The eye started to ache him, and he told Donna that he wanted to go to bed early. She understood and said, "Just let us know when you want to go home". They stayed at the soda shop for an hour and then dropped Donna home, and Donny next. He didn't sleep well that night. The eye kept aching him. He couldn't wait for morning to come. His whole body ached that morning. He took another hot shower, ate a good breakfast, and asked Steve what the plans were for the day.

Chapter XVI

"Barbara and I were planning to go watch the Cubs play at Wrigley Field, and you and Donna are welcome to come with us. "Great", said Donny, "but you have to lend me a few bucks until I get to the bank on Monday". The only seats available that day were in the bleachers. They enjoyed the hot sun, and they all go sunburned. Donny wore his Cubs hat, which help the sun from his cut. When the game was over, they stopped at a restaurant for a hamburger and coke, and then proceeded home.

In a week Father Joe was planning on leaving for his new assignment in New York, but he told the kids that he would be down at the hall on Friday to say good-bye. Barbara came up with an excellent going-away present for him. She got all the kids that came to the hall together one day, and they had their picture taken in front of the church. She had the picture blown up and had it framed. When Father Joe came to the hall on Friday, two days before he was to leave, Barbara brought the picture with her. Father Joe made a nice speech, and had tears in his eyes when he finished. Barbara handed him the picture and he choked up. He told the kids that he would miss them all and would say a prayer for each of them daily. "The picture will be on my dresser and I will look at it daily", Father Joe said. He went around and shook everyone's hand, but when he got to Steve and Donny, he gave them a big hug. The same with Barbara, and then he left. Most of the kids had tears in their eyes, while some like Barbara wept openly.

The next day, Donny came down for breakfast and was surprised when he walked into the kitchen. His Mom, Dad and Steve were standing in front of the birthday cake. It was the first time in weeks that he had forgotten about his birthday. The phone rang, and it was Donna and Barbara singing Happy Birthday to him. He thanked them and told Donna he would see her later. He put the receiver down and turned to his family. Donny said, "Now that I'm 18, I have decided to join the Navy. I don't want to wait every day for the mail to come. I don't want to wait for my greetings from the Army and go into the infantry. In the Navy I may have some options. I hope you understand, Mom and Dad".

John looked at his son and told him that they do understand and support him in his decision. "When do you plan to enlist", asked

John. "As soon as Steve can drop me off there. All I need to take with me is my toothbrush and a few dollars to buy something in the commissary store on the base. I looked into this all week", he said. Mary held back the tears, knowing all along this day would come. Donny got himself ready, kissed his Mom and Dad, hugged and kissed Donna, and said he would write her as soon as he got settled in. He gave Barbara a hug and told her to watch out for Steve, since he would not be there to do it. He then looked at Steve, pulled him into a big hug and started to choke up, saying, "Take care, my big brother. I'll see you soon". He started to cry as he left them and refused to look back.

He got to the door and went in. "Am I doing the right thing", he thought to himself. As he walked in, the place was empty, except for a chief petty officer at the desk. Donny approached him and told him he was ready to enlist. He filled out some papers and went into another room, where he saw two enlistees in their shorts, getting examined by a corpsman. They took Donny's blood pressure, a urine specimen, and then checked him over. The whole exam took less than a half-hour, and he was found to be in good shape. Donny and three other recruits were taken to a train. They boarded and were on their way to Great Lakes Training Center.

The train ride took about an hour; they then boarded a bus, which took them through the main gates of the training center, and drove to a large building where a chief petty officer met them and welcomed them. They all exited the bus and were marched into the building, which was a gymnasium used by the Navy personnel on the base. Once inside, they were told to sit down on the gym floor. The chief told them that they no longer were civilians; you now belong to the United States Navy and you will do as I say. "I am now your Mommy and Daddy. The first thing we will do is go next door and get you some clothes and things, then come back here and stencil the clothes". They all got up and marched single file into the warehouse. They were first given a duffel bag to put all the clothes into. The men behind the counters asked the recruits their sizes, and they sometimes got the right size.

Sheets and pillowcases were the next articles they were given. Next came underwear, white and black socks, dress whites, and dungaree shirts and bell-bottom trousers, a pair of black shoes, leggings, followed by a pea coat. Everything was put into the duffel bag. The last item given out was the stencil. Last names were stenciled and blank ink and a brush were given to them. They all waited outside when finished, and when the last man came out, they were then marched into the gym. The stenciling took over an hour. Then they were marched to a barracks, which they were told would be Home Sweet Home for them for the next nine weeks. They were assigned bunks. In front of the bunks were wooden boxes and they had better be neat. They were then shown how to make their beds. They were told to put the sheets on. "I want those sheets as tight as possible", said the chief. "I want to have a coin bounce on the bed"!

"Oh, boy', thought Donny. "Mom should see me now"! Donny never made his bed at home. Most of the recruits never did. They would learn, the chief always said. When everyone was finished, they were told to go outside and then they would go and eat. They lined up and marched to the mess hall. By this time, everyone was hungry and tired. Donny was surprised at how good the food was and how large the portions were. It was an early night for the boys, lights out at 9:00 pm. "Tomorrow will be a busy day", said the chief. "You will be examined by a doctor and a dentist and you will get shots, a haircut, and be given a schedule of the classes you will attend while being here. I promise you this will be no picnic", he said. "I want you all to write to your parents at least once a week. A diagram of the base will also be given to you, so study it. Combination locks will be passed out and put on your storage boxes. No one is to go into any other boxes than their own. Good night, gentlemen".

Donny thought it was the middle of the night when the lights in the barracks came on and someone yelled, "Everyone up"! Donny thought it was way too early to get up, when someone who was ignoring the order yelled, "Time to shut the lights off"! Next came the banging of garbage cans and the chief's loud voice saying to be outside for inspection in a half-hour. Mike, the boy who had the bunk above Donny, jumped down and cried, "Get up, boy! He means business. You don't want to get on the wrong side of him now"! "But it's so early", cried Donny. "You're in the Navy now, my boy, so get up. I'll help you make your bed while you go and shower". After showering, he got dressed and went outside, standing next to Mike and said, "Thanks, Mike. I owe you one".

The chief did a roll call and said, "Well, we haven't lost anyone yet". They then marched to the mess hall for breakfast, the main dish being chipped beef on toast. Donny took a liking to it, which wasn't at all appetizing. After breakfast, the boys lined up and did calisthenics for a half-hour. The chief then took them for a run around the track, telling they that they would increase the distance each day. The chief reminded Donny of Douglas MacArthur because of the way he wore his hat and even smoked a corncob pipe. Next was the doctor's visit where they were checked and then got their shots. They then proceeded to the dentist, where Donny found out he had a couple of small cavities, which were taken care of. It was lunchtime then, and they all marched to the mess hall. Donny wasn't hungry but ate a little, and then came the dreaded haircuts. Donny had a lot of hair when he got in the barber's chair, but was almost bald when the barber got through with him. It was the joke of the day to see everyone come outside and line up by the building. "Those barbers are real jokers", thought Donny.

They were all given old Springfield rifles that had the firing pin removed and would be used for close order drill each morning. The chief told them that if they got good enough with rifle drills, they could go into competition with other units. "Looking at the likes of you", the chief said, "I would be happy to see you just carry the rifles. Tomorrow you will be firemen, but now I want you all to go into the barracks and write your parents. Tell them what a good time you are having in camp. The smoking lamp is lit, which means you can smoke in the barracks. We will meet outside at 17:30 for dinner".

Chapter XVII

Donny went into the barracks and headed for his bunk. His first letter would be to his parents, letting them know that he was adjusting just fine to Navy life. He goes to bed early but doesn't like the idea of getting up before 7:00 am. He mentioned his friend, Mike, who makes sure he gets up on time and hangs out with him whenever they have some free time, which they don't have much of. Mike lives in Chicago, but closer to the south side. He told them the food is good and he is putting on weight. "I'm not sure you would recognize me", he said, "with my baldy haircut. The barbers take pleasure in cutting the recruits' hair". He made the letter short and to the point. He next letter was to Donna.

He started out by telling her he missed her very much. He told her about Mike, and said that maybe when they came home on leave the six of them could go out on the town. Mike got engaged before he enlisted and plans on getting married after his enlistment. "You will like him when you meet him". There was an Out mail box in the barracks near the door, which saved them a long walk to the post office on the base. Donny dropped the two letters in the Out box. He now would wait for the answer to his letters.

Mike was still writing, so he just sat down on his bunk, thinking of home. He was starting to feel a little homesick, when Mike jumped down from his bunk with letter in his hand, heading for the Out box. When he got back, he asked Donny if he wanted to take a walk around the base. "Sure", said Donny, breaking his thoughts of home.

Steve was reading the paper and saw an ad that a policeman's test was coming up. He decided right then that this could be the job for him. The pay was good and the benefits great. It could be the right job with a future, so he filled out an application form, and when the day came for the test, he took it. "Nothing to lose, but plenty to gain", he thought. One thing bothered him. Most of his friends had been drafted; some were in basic training, yet he hadn't been called for the draft yet. "Maybe the quota has been filled", he thought. He started to think about his future, and wanted Barbara in it. So he went to a jewelry store and bought a ring. He knew Barbara loved him, and he hoped she was ready for the next step, to be his wife.

That evening he took her out to dinner at a restaurant they liked to go to before going to the hall on Friday. While they waited for the waiter to come to take their order, Steve proceeded to tell Barbara how much he cared for, and he told her that he wanted to spend the rest of his life with her. He pulled out the ring and said, "You can make me the happiest person on earth if you will marry me". He took her hand and slipped the ring on her finger. "Oh, Steve", she cried, "yes, yes, I'll marry you". She got up, thinking they were alone, and flew into his open arms. "I love you so much", she said. The few people in the restaurant who witnessed the occasion started applauding. Steve looked up at the people and said, "She said yes, she will marry me". Barbara looked down at the ring and said, "Steve, it's beautiful. Oh how I love you". Their appetites satisfied, Steve said, "Let's go, sweetheart". When they got into the car, Barbara said, "Let's go to my house and show my Mom and Dad. I love you so much", she said, as she snuggled close to him.

Barbara was all excited. She couldn't wait to show Mom the ring. When they walked into the house, Frank and Rose were at the kitchen table, talking. Barbara walked in and cried out, "Look, Mom and Dad, we're engaged", flashing the ring back and forth. "Congratulations", said Rose, while Frank shook Steve's hand. "Welcome to our family", Frank said. Rose got up and gave Steve a hug and a kiss.

Mary doesn't come down to the store downstairs except maybe to clean up, but today she had something to ask John. He was at the sewing machine when she entered. "Hi honey", she said. "Oh", thought John, "am I in trouble"? Mary said, "I have been thinking. I want you to teach me how to drive". "Why", he said, "Don't I take you wherever you want to go?" "Yes", she said, "but if I could drive, I could save you all that time by shopping while you are working. I want you to teach me, John". He knew she would get her way, so why fight it. "OK", he said, "how about we start after dinner tonight?" "Great", Mary replied. "I'll be ready".

Steve wrote and told Donny about getting engaged and he would like Donny to be his best man when they get married. No date had been set. They are still trying to come up with one. He also told Donny that he took the policeman's test, which wasn't that tough. Donny was happy for his brother and Barbara, and he got out his stationery and started to write Steve and tell him how happy he was for the two of them. He also told him that he thought that he would make a great cop.

Frank and Rose were thrilled with their daughter getting engaged. They both knew that Steve would always be there for their daughter.

The classes at the training center started, and Donny was enjoying the lessons. He wondered if maybe life on a ship was his calling, or if he should go for the Frogmen, which is the elite of the Navy. He thought he would enjoy sailing to different ports and seeing how other people lived, but then again he thought it was a little too early to decide his future in the Navy. I'll wait until I graduate boot camp. By then I'll see what course I will take. His thoughts were interrupted by the voice of the chief. "Are you with us, Donny", he cried out. "Yes, sir", he replied. "Tomorrow we will go out to the rifle range and teach you how to fire a rifle'. Donny had never fired a gun in his life, and this was a new experience for him. They were shown how to hold the rifle in different positions of firing. He watched as man after man took turns firing at a target. When his name was called, he stepped forward, took the rifle, aimed and fired. He missed the target completely, and the boy in the pit put up a flag called "Maggie's Drawers". This showed a complete miss. He tried two more times, and again Maggie's Drawers were shown.

An instructor, watching Donny's misses, came up to him and showed him the proper way to shoot. Donny put the rifle closer to his eye and fired. He hit the target, but the kick of the rifle split his lip. The instructor was at Donny's side again, handing him a napkin to wipe the blood off his lip. He showed Donny again, and this time he fired and got a bull's eye. His next four shots were all close together near the bull's eye. Donny was happy with himself, forgetting his bloody lip.

The next step was firing a 45 pistol, but this time he could not get the hang of it and fired off five shots, barely grazing the target.

The base was having an open house for the families of the recruits, and it was held on Sunday from 11:30 am until 3:00 pm. They were all handed directions, and a map of the base to send to their families. Steve drove his parents and the two girls there. It was a warm and sunny day, and a nice day for a drive. Donny met them at the parking lot, and it was a joyful, tearful reunion. The boys walked around the base, holding hands with the girls, while the parents walked behind.

They stopped at the commissary and had cold drinks, while the girls bought their parents souvenirs. Mary kept taking pictures, and used up two rolls. Donny told them that he would be graduating and coming home for a week or two. The time few, and it was getting near to 3:00 pm closing time. Donny, his parents, and the two girls walked over to the parking lot. They said their good-byes and left.

Donny, feeling homesick again, walked the two blocks to his barracks. When he got to his bunk, he noticed Mike writing letters in his bunk. Mike told him that his parents couldn't make it, and his fiancée doesn't drive, "but thank goodness we will be going home on leave soon", he said.

Chapter XVIII

The following morning, after they had breakfast and lined up outside their barracks, they were marched to a small red building. They were given gas masks and instructed on how to use them. They were told to put on the masks, and then marched inside. They were told to sit down on the wooden seats in the building. When the siren sounded, they were told to remove their gas masks and walk out in a single file, holding their gas masks in their hands. The shrill sound of the siren shook then all, and they proceeded to remove their gas masks and walked out the side door. They were all choking and rubbing their eyes from inhaling some of the gas. Outside was a barrel of cold water that they all headed for, washing out their eyes. The eyes stung for about an hour, and the taste of the gas longer.

Mary was proceeding with her driving lessons, but as yet she didn't drive on the main roads. John was taking her through driving at a slow pace. Mary was having problems with the clutch pedal. She could not adjust to shifting gears and bringing up the clutch. The car kept lurching forward and then stalling. John would come in the house after driving with her and head for the medicine cabinet and pop two aspirins into his mouth.

Then finally at one lesson, it happened. She put the car in gear and it moved smoothly and she finally got the hang of it. She wanted to cry out in joy when it became easy for her. The shifting was accomplished and John noticed he had no more headaches. John felt good about teaching Mary, but knew that this could never be his profession. His nerves could never take it.

Mary was ready for her test and he drove her down there. The written test was simple enough, and she waited to be called for the driving part of the test. It was a short line and she was called quickly. She drove around the block, parked the car where she was told, and then headed back. She passed the test and got her license, and John also let her drive home. When she got home, she called Eleanor and told her the good news. She then asked Eleanor if she wanted to go shopping. "Here we go", thought John.

Barbara had been taking driving lessons for a long time, and she finally got the courage to take her driving test. She passed with no trouble at all, and now Donna was asking her Dad to teach her. Frank was a good instructor and Donna took to driving like a fish to water. Rose asked him to teach her, but he said she had to wait a little while until his nerves came back to earth. His stomach had been giving him trouble for a while and his doctor told him that he had a nervous stomach, brought on by daily stress. He was told that he was a candidate for an ulcer.

Chapter XIX

Now that Barbara passed her driving test and had her license, she was saving a lot of time by driving her Mom around to the stores, and doing errands for her father. Donna was after Barbara now to teach her how to drive. Barbara told her that once she has experience behind the wheel for a while, she would consider it, but until then she would drive her to places when she had time. Donna agreed, and it was set aside for the time being.

Mary and John were talking about taking a vacation and driving down to Florida. They included Joe and Eleanor in the plans, and the four of them started to plan the trip. John would close down the store for two weeks. This would be the first vacation they would be taking since coming to America. John told Joe that they would have to take turns driving because it's just too long of a trip for one person to drive. Joe agreed, and they discussed driving 400 miles a day, stopping at motels by 9:00 pm. Expenses would be split down the middle. Their destination would be Daytona Beach, where they saw an ad for a model home they wanted to look at and possibly buy for their retirement years. Two weeks would give them sufficient time to get there and look around. They were getting all excited about the trip and talked about it daily. The days flew by, and before long they were out loading the car with luggage and things they would need for the trip. Mary had to bring her own pillows, and soon after, they gassed up and were on their way.

Steve and Barbara were on hand to wish them a safe trip. Joe started out to drive first, and put on 350 miles on the speedometer. They all agreed they would pull into a motel for the day. There was a restaurant next door, and they had dinner and then called it a night. "The first day is always the toughest", said Joe. They went to bed early and got a good night's sleep. They went for a hearty breakfast, gassed up the car, and were ready for the second day, with John taking the wheel. He drove for a few hours, saw a sign for a restaurant and gas, and took a vote to stop for lunch. They all agreed on stopping; they were all getting hungry. After a small lunch, they continued their journey. John drove for a few more hours, and then they saw the signs for Jacksonville, Florida, 20 miles. They found a motel, restaurant and gas, and pulled in. After a good dinner, they walked around for a little while, and then called it a night. The next morning after breakfast they proceeded to

Daytona Beach, arriving there after lunch.

They found the models by asking the gas attendant for directions. The homes were just what they advertised, and they were all in agreement to buy. The homes were being built near the beach. It didn't take them long to sign the contracts, but specified that the homes had to be next to each other. The homes would be up and ready to move into in seven months. They were told that they would be notified for their inspection. They picked out their lots and put down the down payment. They celebrated that evening and couldn't waiting for the homes to be built. They all slept well, and the next day they were back looking at their homes. The drove around the area, looking at all the restaurants and new stores being built. They talked about coming back when the homes were finished. Joe said that in Chicago they may have snow, but there the temperature would be in the 80's. "Wow", said Mary, "won't that be wonderful".

The last day of their vacation was spent on the beach, not far from where their new home was going to be built. The four of them were talking, daydreaming, and not realizing how hot the sun was. They all got sunburned. That afternoon they spent sitting on the patio, trying to catch some of the cool breezes from the ocean. They went to the store and bought three jars of Noxzema to cool off the burn. Joe told John that if they wanted to, they could leave in the morning and get home in two days, stopping in a motel only once. "Fine with me", said John. They asked their wives and they, too, agreed. They spent the next few hours packing up, and loaded the car. Then they went out to dinner. John had a bad night; the sunburn kept him awake. When Joe saw him, he told him that he'd better drive first. John didn't object, thinking he could rest up before he took the wheel. They drove for a short time, stopped for breakfast and gassed up the car. Joe continued driving, and after 400 miles of driving, John told him he felt good enough to take over. They stopped at a rest stop, stretched their legs, got gas and John took over. When dusk approached, they started looking for a motel for the night. They saw a sign that read Motel and Gas ten miles, which they were happy to see.

They all agreed to pull into the motel for the night, being seven hours from home. After a good dinner, they all felt tired and called it a night. They were up by 7:00 am, got breakfast and gassed up and were on their final stretch home. John said that he would drive the rest of the way. They were twenty minutes from home when, out of nowhere, came this car trying to pass them and blew a tire. The car went out of control and slammed into John's side of the car, just behind the driver's seat. Joe caught a glimpse of the car just before it hit and screamed, "Look out, we're going to be hit"! All four of them were hurt and pinned in the wreckage. The fire department was close by and was there in a few minutes. They had to cut parts of the car away to get Joe and the wives free. An ambulance came and took them to the hospital, which was a short distance away. John was still pinned in the front seat, and it took close to a half-hour to free him. The driver of the other car was drunk, and put into a police car. He didn't have a scratch on him. He was later handcuffed and taken away.

John, when freed, was taken to the hospital and put in critical care. Eleanor had a cut on the eyebrow, was stitched up and released. Her husband, Joe, was unconscious and was wheeled into the X-ray room. Mary had a broken rib and cuts on her face. She was conscious and kept asking for her husband. She, too, was taken for X-rays. Eleanor called a neighbor who picked her up. She was told that Joe had no broken bones, just a few cuts and whiplash, and they put a collar on his neck. He would be released shortly. Mary was advised to stay in the hospital overnight because of her head injury. John, the most seriously hurt, had a concussion and back injuries. A neurologist was called in to examine him.

Chapter XX

As Mary was being attended to, she kept pleading with the doctor to please call her son, Steve. "He has to be told", she cried out. She was squirming so much that the doctor finally told the nurse in the room to please get her son's number and call him so that he can suture her face. Mary gave the nurse Steve's number and thanked her. The doctor looked at Mary and said, "Now may I stitch your cuts"?

The nurse told Steve who she was and told him about the accident. She explained that she didn't know the extent of the injuries, but told him that his mother was doing fine. He thanked her and hung up. He called Barbara and told her about the phone call and said he was going to the hospital. Barbara said she would go with him. "While waiting, I'll call the Red Cross and see if they can get a hold of Donny". "Good", he said, "I'll be right over". When they got to the hospital, they were told that their conditions haven't changed, but that his mother is fine and will be kept overnight for observation. He went to his mother's room and found her sitting up in bed. "Oh, Steve", she cried when she saw him. "It was horrible". "How is Dad", she asked. "We don't know. The last we heard he had back injuries and is in a coma". "Oh God", she said. "I just don't know'.

Steve went to give his Mom a hug, but she flinched and said, "I have some ribs broken, but they will mend. How will Donny know", she asked. "Barbara called the Red Cross. They will notify him". Steve found his father's room, and found him with weights on a pulley strapped to his legs. John was in a coma, so Steve bent over his Dad and kissed him on the forehead and whispered, "Get well, Dad; I love you'.

He then checked in on Uncle Joe who was in the X-ray room. Aunt Eleanor was in his room, waiting for him to come down. When she saw Steve, she broke down and started to sob. Steve gave her a hug, and then asked how she and Uncle Joe were. "I'm fine", she said, "and have been released. My neighbor is on his way to pick me up. Uncle Joe's in the X-ray room. He has a broken ankle and possibly a broken shoulder. He may have to stay in the hospital, depending on the results of the X-ray". Steve and Barbara said their good-byes and went back to see his mother. They stayed awhile, and then told his mother that they have to leave to see if Donny had been contacted. He said he'd be back in the morning. When they got home, Barbara called the Red Cross and was told that Donny was on his way home by train. The tickets were supplied to him. They told Barbara his destination and time of arrival. Barbara thanked him, and a short time later Donny called. He was at the station and would wait for Steve to pick him up. Steve told him to have something to eat, and by then they would be there. "Fine", said Donny. Donny was in the waiting room when Steve came. They gave each other a hug, and then Donny wanted to know all about the accident and how everyone was. He wanted to go to the hospital right then, but Steve said it would be best to wait until morning and let their parents get some rest. "They may have some good new then", he said. Donny agreed, and they dropped Barbara home. Neither boy slept much that night, worried about their parents. Steve and Donny went to the hospital alone. They felt it would be best, and the girls understood.

Mary was up and dressed, waiting for her sons to come. The hospital was releasing her. She met the boys at the elevator. She kissed and hugged them, and then told Donny of the horror of the crash. Donny helped his Mom, and asked how his Dad was. "He's still in a coma', she said. "We won't know until he comes out of it". Mary told the boys that she would be going home with them. "There isn't anymore that they can do for me. The ribs will heal in time". After visiting Uncle Joe who has to remain in the hospital for a little longer, they looked in on their Dad. He was all strapped in with tubes in him and the pulley above his legs. They talked to him as if he could hear them, and Mary cried. They said their good-byes after a short time, with Steve saying he'd bring the car up to the front entrance for his mother. The nurse wheeled out Mary in a wheelchair, and when she got to the front door, Steve and Donny took over, helping their Mom to the car. On the way home, Mary told them about their home they had purchased in Florida for their retirement. She then stopped and realized what she had said, and started to cry. "Mom", cried Donny, "It's OK. Dad will be just fine; he's a fighter".

When they got home, the phone rang and Steve answered it. Barbara asked them all over for dinner, which she made. Steve asked his Mom, and she said OK. They spent a few hours there, enjoying the southern fried chicken dinner Barbara made. Mary was getting tired, so she apologized to the Young's and thanked Barbara for the delicious meal that she made. She really did enjoy their company. Mary mentioned the home they bought in Daytona Beach. It wasn't far from the home the Young's own in Florida. When Mary got home she went straight to bed, taking a sleeping pill that the doctor had prescribed for her.

Mary was all dressed, waiting for Steve to take her to the hospital. Steve was ready, but was waiting for Donny, who was on the phone with Donna. "Let's go, Donny", said Steve. "Mom is waiting". Donny told Donna he had to leave, but would see her later in the day. He then hung up the phone. The ride to the hospital was only twenty minutes without traffic, but today traffic was heavy. When they got to John's room, there was a neurosurgeon in the room, looking at John's records. "Hello", he said. "I'm Dr. Sorretto. I just looked over your husband's records and X-rays, and I feel that it's crucial that we operate as soon as he comes out of the coma. I'm sure he will soon. If we don't operate, he will be in a wheelchair for the rest of his life". He showed Mary the X-rays and explained the procedure. He told her that there are certain risks, but he said John looks like he is in excellent shape and hasn't neglected his body. The only vice my husband has", Mary said, "is that he smokes a few cigarettes a day". Mary signed the papers for the operation, after talking it over with the boys. They stayed in the room for about an hour. Mary kept holding John's hand, talking to him and watching for any movement from him. At times it looked as if John understood every word Mary was saying. When they left the room, Mary gave John a kiss.

They went to Joe's room and found Eleanor there visiting him. Mary told them about the operation John is going to face. "He's a tough guy", said Joe, who was going to be released soon. Mary got a page over the loudspeaker. She grabbed a house phone and called the number given to her. She was told that John has awakened from his coma, and was told to go to his room. "Oh, my God", she cried. "John came out of his coma. We have to go to John's room now", Mary said. They told Joe and Eleanor that they would see them later. The three of them rushed to John's room as fast as they could, and when they got to his room, John was being propped up by two nurses. When he saw Mary walk into the room, he gave her a big smile. She walked over to him and kissed him and said, "Hi, honey. You sure gave us a scare". The boys were standing behind Mary, waving their hands and smiling. "Hi, boys", said John. It came out mumbled, but they both understood.

The doctor walked into the room, checked John out, and said that they would operate tomorrow after a few more X-rays and tests. The doctor told Mary that he would call her as soon as the operation was over, and for her to go home and wait there instead of the hospital waiting room. "OK", said Mary, "But please take good care of him". "I love you, John", she said, as she left the room with her two sons. When they got home, Mary laid down on the couch and fell asleep, but was jolted up by the phone. It was the doctor, telling Mary that they had moved up the operation after reviewing the X-rays and other tests. The operation was scheduled to begin in a few hours. He told Mary he would call her the minute the operation was over.

Steve called Barbara and told her that the operation was moved up to tonight. She told Steve that she and Donna would be right over to keep them company. Frank had bought his daughter a used late-model car when she passed her driving test. On the way to their house, Barbara stopped and picked up a pizza, knowing that none of them ate anything all day. After they ate, they sat down in the living room and turned on the television. No one really knew what was on the TV; they were all in a state of shock waiting for the phone to ring.

At 10:00 pm they shut off the television and talked. Steve told Barbara that she should go home, knowing that she gets up early. He told her that he would call her the minute he got any news. She hesitated, but at 11:30 she said she had better go, but told Steve to make sure he called her no matter what time it was. He promised her he would. Mary thanked Barbara for coming and also for the pizza. It was 1:30 am when the phone rang, and Mary and the boys jumped up from the couch, half-asleep. Mary picked up the phone. It was the doctor, telling her that the operation when well and John came through great. He is now in the recovery room and will be put into this own room in an hour. "The prognosis is good', he said. "Now get a good night's sleep and you can see your husband in the morning". "Thank you very much, doctor", said Mary, and hung up the receiver. "Daddy came though the operation very well", she told the boys. "He has to go to rehabilitation for awhile, but thank

God he will be fine". Both boys got up and hugged their mother, and then they all had a good cry. Steve looked at the time, but he promised Barbara that he would call, so he did. Frank answered the phone, and Steve told him, "I'm sorry about the time, but I promised Barbara that I would call her about my Dad". Frank told him that he understood and would get Barbara. She was up in a second when her Dad said it was Steve. "The doctor called and said the operation was successful and that my Dad will be OK', Steve said. "Oh, that's great news, honey", she said. "I want to go with you to visit him tomorrow", she said. "OK, said Steve, "I love you", and the phone went dead. Mary and the boys finally got a good night's sleep. It was as if a weight was lifted from their shoulders.

John was propped up in bed when Mary, the boys and the girls walked into his room. Mary couldn't believe how good he looked after what he went through. He was on pain medication, which was doing a good job. John said the nurses had him up on his feet for a few minutes, and it sure felt great. "I hope that I will start walking soon". "With your strong will, John, you will be running soon", said Mary. "I hope so", he said. "I heard that they arrested the guy that hit us. He was drunk and was giving the cops a hard time. I hope they throw the book at him", said John.

The doctor was in in the morning. Donny told him that he had to head back to the base before they start looking for him. "OK", said John. "It was nice of the Navy to give you the time off". Steve told Donny that he would drive him back to the base with Barbara and Donna. Donny said, "How about leaving before noon tomorrow, if that's OK with everyone". They all agreed and said that they would leave about 11:00 am. Mary and the kids said their good-byes and Steve told his Dad that they would see him in the afternoon tomorrow. After a hug and a few kisses, they all left. On the way home Barbara invited them for dinner. "My Mom and Dad insisted on it", she said. After a good meal, Mary felt that she was being spoiled and will have a tough time getting back to cooking. Rose said it was great having the family there, and hoped they enjoyed it.

The trip to Great Lakes training center took an hour and a half because of heavy traffic. "I hope you can come to my graduation in three more weeks", Donny said to Donna as they waited in traffic.

"I wouldn't miss it", she said, and then asked "Do you know where you are going after graduation"? "No", said Donny, "but I may try out for the Frogmen. They are the Navy elite. It's hard to get in, but I figure I have nothing to lose by trying". Barbara turned her head to look at Donny and said, "Isn't it dangerous"? What is dangerous, you can get killed driving your car". "I guess so", said Barbara. They finally arrived at the center, and Donny showed the guard at the gate his papers, and Steve was permitted to proceed to Donny's barracks. After getting his duffel bag out of the trunk. They all said their good-byes and Donny went into his barracks.

Mike was the first to see him, and welcomed him back. "I was sorry to hear about your Dad's accident. How is he doing"? "He was operated on and is now in rehab, doing well". "Good", said Mike. "I missed you". Donny stated to unpack and said, "Thanks, Mike".

After Steve dropped the girls home, he proceeded back to his house. He gave his Mom a kiss hello, and then noticed the letter on the table. "Oh", he said, as he noticed who the letter came from. He opened the letter as fast as he could. He saw the first sentence: "You are requested to appear at the U.S. Army induction center, downtown Chicago, at 9:00 am on Friday, August 3, 1942". His day was ruined. He quickly called Barbara and told her the bad news. "Oh no", she cried out, "the Army is going to ruin our plans for the future". "I don't think this war will last too much longer", said Steve. "We have the Germans on the run now, and maybe they will surrender soon". "Oh Steve, I sure hope it ends quickly".

When they went to the hospital, they found John sitting up, looking out the window watching the cars in the hospital parking lot. Mary gave him a kiss, and asked if he had rehab today. "Yes", said John, "and they took me down to the gym. The put me between parallel bars, had me hold on, and I walked the whole length. It ached a little but it sure felt good". Steve got his Dad's attention, and said, "I got drafted today and have to report to the induction center on Friday". "I'm sorry to hear that, son', said John. "Well", said Steve, "I might as well get it over with". After leaving John, they stopped in to see Joe. Eleanor was there and the bandage on her head was missing, showing a large wound that was in the process of healing. She said that Joe was being released in two more days.

Friday came, and Barbara was there to take Steve downtown to the induction center. He was given a physical, passed, and was sworn in. He was taken by train to Ft. Sheridan for two weeks of processing. After all the testing, he was then taken by train to Arkansas, an artillery center, for three days. He was then sent to Ft. Sill in Oklahoma for forward artillery observation training. He spent sixteen weeks in training, and was then given a two-week furlough. He wrote Barbara and told her the day he would be coming home so that she could pick him up at the train station. He was sitting in the lobby, close to the main entrance, when Barbara walked in. They saw each other almost at the same time, and ran to each other. Steve gained a few pounds, but on him it was all muscle. He was now sporting a moustache, which was neatly trimmed, but Barbara didn't like it and told him it had to go. He laughed and said he didn't like it either and planned to shave it off as soon as he got home.

Chapter XXI

Barbara drove Steve to his home where he was met by Mary, sitting on the front stoop of the house. She laughed when she saw the moustache and said, "Is this my son"? Steve told her that it's going as soon as he gets a razor to his face. "You look so much older with it on", she said. After a hug and a kiss, they proceeded indoors. How is Dad doing", asked Steve. "He's doing just great, and walking with a can now. The doctor said that he should be released from the hospital this weekend. Uncle Joe and Aunt Eleanor are home now, but Uncle Joe still needs a cane to get around".

After dinner they took a ride to the hospital, and Steve still didn't shave. He wanted his Dad's opinion on the moustache. John said he like the moustache, or just said he did to make Steve feel good. The three of them took a walk around the hospital, with John showing them the gym where he has therapy. He uses a walker, but hopes to get rid of that and just use a cane. John said that he plans to reopen the store in two more weeks. "Don't rush it, Dad", said Steve. "Do you have any orders where you will be going when you get back", asked John. "No, just rumors, Dad", said Steve. "Everyone thinks that we will be going overseas and try to end this war. General Eisenhower thinks we are close to ending it soon". "I sure hope so", said John. "Is there any chance of the hospital releasing you while I'm home on leave", asked Steve. "I'll ask the doctor tomorrow when he pays me a visit", said John.

The next morning, while he was getting dressed to go see Barbara, the phone rang, and he heard his mother say, "Oh, that's great, John. We will be there soon". She looked at Steve and said, "Daddy is being released this morning". "Great", said Steve. "I'll call Barbara and tell her we will pick her up on the way". "Fine", said Mary. When they got to the hospital and entered John's room, he was all dressed and ready to go. The doctor told him to use a walker while he is home for better support until he gets strong enough to use a can. He was to have therapy at home for at least a month. A nurse finally came with a wheelchair and wheeled him to the front entrance where Steve met them. Barbara went out ahead and brought the car to the front while Steve and Mary helped him into the front seat. John asked if he could drive, and Steve said, "Soon, Dad, soon".

Some of the neighbours were out in front of their house to greet John home. When he exited the car, they yelled, "Welcome home, John'. He looked over at them and said, "It's great to be home".

Chapter XXII

Graduation at Great Lakes Training Center was fast approaching. Donny went and talked to his chief petty officer about his decision to try out for the Frogmen. The chief, being in the Navy for 20 years, told Donny that he would see what he could do for him. Donny was thrilled when he got the invitation to go there and try out. No guarantees he was told. Donny passed the written test with no problem. Next was the pool. He stayed in the water for most of the day. It was tough, but Donny was determined to give it all he had. He was told that 70% of the applicants drop out after the first day. He made it through the first day, achy all over, but he was ready for the second day. It was back in the water. Donny loved the water, but he was getting concerned after four days of swimming on top and under and let up. They were pushed to near exhaustion. After a full week of near exhaustion and pain in every joint, he was sent back to his unit to await word. Everyone asked him the same question, including the chief. "How did you do"? He didn't know and said that he would be contacted.

Donny felt and looked completely exhausted. He wanted to sleep for a week. "No way", said the chief. "We have graduation exercises to do, and we are behind schedule, so be ready and out on the parade grounds in half an hour. "Oh nuts", he said, but took a fast shower, changed clothes, and was out on the parade grounds in 20 minutes. Donny looked around and saw that the whole battalion was out there with another ten battalions practicing. The bands were all out there and they sounded very good. Graduation day came and Donny was informed by the chief, handing him a letter, telling him he had made the Frogmen program. After two weeks leave, he was told to report to classes. He was told that only 40% made it through the first week. Donny wasn't that surprised about the percentage ration of only 40% making the first week. It will be a tough program, but he felt determined that he would go all the way to get into the Frogman unit.

On graduation day Mary, John, Joe and Eleanor left early to beat the traffic. They gave themselves three hours to make the trip, and stopping for lunch was in the plan. Joe would do the driving, and if he got tired, Mary could take over. Not that she was looking forward to it. Barbara, Donna and their parents also went. Busia wasn't up to it. She came down with a cold and figured it best to stay home. It was beautiful, warm sunny day, and the graduation went perfectly. Families met other families after the ceremonies on the parade ground. Donny told everyone about his going to Frogmen School after a two-week leave, which all the men were happy to hear about, but none of the women showed any emotion. Donna, who got her driving license a week before, told Donny that she would drive him home if it was OK with his parents. Donny was happy about going home, but more excited about going to Frogmen School.

Chapter XXIII

After Steve's furlough, which he felt went much too fast, he flew to California to a U.S. embarkation Center for one week, and was then put on a ship, destination unknown. After a few days of sailing, the ship came upon a storm, near Cape Hatteras. They went through the Bermuda Triangle without any problems except heavy rains and waves 10 feet high. Many of the sailors on board, plus most of the soldiers, got seasick. Steve felt lucky that he didn't get sick. The storm lasted for two days before the nice weather broke through. The sea turned from high waves to a sea of glass once the storm has passed. Everyone on board was happy to see the sun come through the clouds. Flying fish could be seen following the ship, and for many of the soldiers aboard the ship this was a sight that they would write home about. Lookouts on the ship were posted with binoculars, scanning the water for any movement or from any periscopes, which they hoped they wouldn't see. The ship was in a fleet of many warships. It was good to see all those ships. Good protection, Steve thought.

On the fourth day out, a submarine was spotted on radar and an alarm was sounded. The ship went into a zigzag pattern, trying to give the sub a hard target to hit. A few of the destroyers in the fleet went into action and headed for the sub sighting. All of the sailors aboard the ship in the fleet went to their battle stations and were manning their guns. Everyone was in their life jackets. They all knew that the German sub's target was their ship. Steve looked around for his assigned lifeboat, just in case they got hit. The destroyers now were dropping depth charges, which continued for over an hour. It could have been longer, but no one was keeping time. The depth charges finally stopped, and everyone wondered if they had sunk the sub. The ship continued to zigzag for a little while longer, and then went back to its normal course.

Donny was enjoying his leave. Donna took him out for his driving lessons, and in no time at all he got his license., That weekend he went out with Uncle Joe and bought himself a car. On Friday, Donny and the two girls went to the hall. He missed not seeing Father Joe there, but everything else was the same. The record player came on, and the first song was Tennessee Waltz. Donna dragged Donny onto the dance floor. Donna was singing to him as they danced, and he was really enjoying himself. Even his dancing improved. After the hall closed,

Donny told Dona to skip the soda shop because he wanted to be alone with her. They went to her house and watched some television. Donny told her that he would like to spend the rest of his life with her, but if something should happen to him, he didn't want to leave her a widow. He continued to say that he thought it best that they wait until he comes home for good before they make any plans for the future. "Stop it, Donny", she said. "I don't want to hear anymore about you dying and for the life of me, I can't understand why you joined the Frogmen. Why can't you be like anyone else and be put on a ship, serve your country that way, and come home in one piece? Why are you trying to be a hero? You don't have to prove anything to me", she cried. He tried to answer her but he couldn't. He took her in his arms and the two cried like little children until Frank walked in on them and asked Donna what was wrong. "Nothing, Daddy", she said. "We were just talking about this stupid war".

The German sub that was spotted earlier had reappeared, and the destroyers went into action, heading for the latest sub sighting. Steve and the rest of the solders and sailors went into battle stations and put on their life jackets. "Here we go again", thought Steve. The ship went into a zigzag pattern, trying to confuse the sub. As the German sub captain sent out a message to his command post, giving the fleet's position, a depth charge exploded near the sub to cause serious leaks. The sub had to surface to periscope depth, giving the captain of the sub ample time to fire off two torpedoes right at the troop ship. The sub received a direct hit from the destroyers and headed for the bottom to be crushed like an egg. The two torpedoes headed for Steve's ship. One torpedo missed completely, while the other hit the ship in the bow, rocking the whole ship. The force of the explosion knocked Steve to the ground, and when he looked up, he saw the bow of the ship on fire. Sailors were rushing past him to man the fire hoses. It didn't take long for the crew to put out the fire, but the black smoke was getting Steve sick.

Word came over the loudspeakers that the destroyers had sunk the sub, but they sustained enough damage to the bow that they would be heading home for repairs. The ship was still smoking when word came to get to battle stations again., Four German planes were spotted heading their way. "Oh no", cried Steve, "not again". The ship's crew was rushing to their gun turrets to engage the enemy planes. The carrier in the fleet put their planes in the air, and it was a welcome sight to see. Steve had a ringside seat to watch the air battle, which didn't last too long. One German plane was on fire, and the pilot bailed out, while the other three took off, not wanting any contact with the American fliers.

The ship was heading for Norfolk, Virginia, for urgent repairs. One destroyer would accompany the ship in case of any more attacks from the sea or air. They would be sitting ducks for submarines or even a fighter plane. The planes from the carrier were on their way back, and deserved a job well done, losing only one plane in the dogfight, but the pilot was plucked from the water. The ship experienced no problems on the way back to Norfolk, and once they docked, they were all given a week's leave. Steve could not wait to get home and tell his parents and Barbara about the battle they were in.

The months slowly passed, and D-Day was coming. Steve was part of the invasion, but they went ashore after the Allies secured the beaches. As he went ashore, he saw the aftermath, and right there he thanked God he was not in the first wave hitting the beaches. He saw many dead and the wounded being put on boats and taken to the ships. He got sick to his stomach, as did most of his platoon. He looked at the Atlantic wall that the Germans put up and said that no one could land on their beaches without being pushed back to the sea. "Well", he thought, "they sure underestimated the Americans and their Allies.

A large clothing store was opening up three blocks from John's store and this concerned him. How could he compete with such a large store? He was sure he could not meet their prices. Will he lose many of his customers? "Time will tell", he thought. The money Busia gave him was almost used up, but he did have a savings account. How long could he keep up before all the money was gone? He would not tell Mary because he thought it would worry her.

One day Joe stopped in the store and told him he would cut down on his rent so John could ride out the tide. John thanked Joe for his generosity but told him to continue the way it was and see how things go.

When the new store opened, they had banners and balloons all over the front of the store. John took a walk past the store and noticed the prices pasted to the front window. "How in the world can I compete with them", he thought. To compete, he could lower some prices, but not have them that low. He would continue the way he was going until he would be forced to close, if that is what was to be. His stomach was in a knot, but he was not going to alarm Mary.

Two weeks went by and John was surprised that there was no change in his customers. No one ever mentioned the other store, and he never brought it up, either. His customers enjoyed coming to his store, to sit down and talk with John about the old day, and discuss their problems. John was an excellent listener, which kept everyone coming and talking to him.

Mary and John were strict Catholics and tried their best to bring up their sons that way. Mary was more involved in church activities than John. She would volunteer for any worthwhile project and then get John involved with her. He never complained because he was happy to see Mary getting involved with the church, since it kept her busy and happy. The pastor in the church mentioned a few times in his sermons that more people should be more like them.

Donny passed the Frogmen course with no problems. He was a natural. He wrote and told Donna about passing the course. Even though he knew she would not get as excited as he was about it, hopefully she would at least be happy for him. Donny was now in his third week as a Frogman, and was proud of himself for staying with it, he was near exhaustion. No way was he going to pack it in. He would make it or die trying he thought to himself. In the last week they started using explosives and learned to set timers. They were dropped off by a small motorboat and then swam to a beach, loaded with obstacles. They would set the explosives and set the timers to the obstacles pointed out to them, and then swim out to the deep water and wait for the motorboat to come by and pluck them out of the water.

They used the buddy system; once inside the boat, they would help to hold a ring out to bring in the remaining Frogmen. Once they were all in the boat, they all would wait for the charges to go off and see the job they did. They would then head back to the safety of their ship. They were told that there is no room for error, and everyone must be experienced in the knowledge of using explosives.

Their lives depended on it. They continued the same routine, using explosives, for over a week, until the commander was satisfied in everyone's performance. A week went by, and the unit was told that they would be going on a mission into an enemy-held island. The commander told them that the unit was ready, and he was proud to be part of the team. He told them that they would be going on a submarine and would leave soon.

At 06:30 Donny and the unit were all out in front of the barracks where roll call was taken. They proceeded to get on the truck that was out in front and ready for them. No one had much to say, and it was that way until they got to the sub base. Rick, the commander, gave them a short speech of how this mission was important. His last comment was "Good luck". "Let's board the sub". For many of the Frogmen, it was the first time on a submarine. Donny boarded and was amazed at the tight quarters the sub had. There were twelve in their group, and they were shown to their compartment. They would stay surfaced for most of the trip, until they neared the island. The food aboard the sub was great, thought Donny, which is why it was hard to get transferred. "They can have it", he thought. It was not for him. He would rather have the freedom to walk around. Writing letters was out of the question. Since they were briefed on this mission, they were confined to the barracks and now confined on the sub. They were told to stay in their compartment until they got to their destination. Many of Donny's teammates played cards or dice, but he was never into gambling, so he slept or just lay in his bunk and thought of Donna.

Chapter XXIV

After two days of boredom, the captain of the sub made an announcement that tomorrow whey would submerge and stay under until they got to their destination. Rick came over to them and went over their assignment and asked if anyone had any questions. A question came up of how long the fuses should be set for and Rick said four hours. He ended by telling them how important clearing the obstacles on the beach was. The Marines will start their invasion early tomorrow morning and the landing craft had to have the beaches cleared for a successful landing. "Good luck and God Speed. I'll see you all on the beach". The sub surfaced and they were at their destination. Rick came in and said, "This is it, boys, we go over the side in five minutes".

All the men scrambled to their feet, go their gear and went topside to get ready to board their small boats. It was a pitch-black night, the moon hiding behind the clouds. The beach was a long distance away, so the men boarded the boat, which would take them halfway to the beach. They all got into the water as they approached the beach. "So far so good", said Tom, the leader of the group. They all strained their eyes as they neared the beach, looking for any Japanese guards. The moon stayed behind the clouds, giving them the edge they wanted. As they neared the obstacles on the beach, they split up in pairs. They went from one obstacle to another, making sure every obstacle had a charge and timer on it. The moon came out of the clouds and shone on two Japanese sentries patrolling the beach. All twelve Frogmen ducked behind any obstacle they would find until the sentries went by.

Tom went around and checked the charges. When he was satisfied, he told the men to leave and head out to meet the boat. Tom and his men swam out of deep water, where they were plucked out of the water by the motorboat. The boat took them to where the sub was to pick them up. A minute passed as they were waiting; when the sub surfaced and looked like a giant whale breaking the water. The crewmen from the sub helped Tom and his men get on board. In two minutes they were all on board, heading for their quarters, while the sub was preparing to dive.

Donny was getting adjusted to submarine life, but he was glad he would be getting off soon. It takes a certain individual to be a submariner, he thought. It wasn't for him. They stayed submerged for two days, and on the third day the captain made an announcement that a Japanese convoy had been spotted with two large troop transports heading to reinforce an enemy-held island. "We have to try to stop them", he said. "Our plan is to get in closer and fire a torpedo at each of the transports and get out of harm's way before the destroyers get a fix on us. The Frogmen were all bunched together in their compartment, awaiting the next word. "Torpedo's away", cried the captain, "and running straight. We go a hit on the first transport, and it is burning. The second transport got a direct hit mid-ship and is heading for Davie Jones' locker" they were told. A large cheer went up until the next words that the enemy destroyers have picked us up and are heading our way. "We will dive as far as we can and try to evade them. Be as quiet as you can, and prepare for depth charge attacks that will come soon".

It didn't take long before the first charge went off and shook the sub. The next two came closer, and the lights went out for a brief moment. Everyone was getting nervous now. "One hit, and we will all drown', Donny thought, as he lay in his bunk, arms stretched, holding on to both sides. The depth charges continued for what seemed like hours, but really were minutes. The captain took the sub further down, exceeding the danger zone. The sub could be crushed like an egg if they go down any further. A half-hour went by and luck seemed to be with them. The destroyers left when an American plane flew by and called in their position.

There was no way the German destroyers were going to stick around and possibly face the American fleet, which they felt were told of their position. The submarine was getting low on battery power and had to surface soon. The captain brought the sub to periscope depth, looking around and finding that the destroyers and the rest of the German ships had left. He surfaced to recharge the sub's batteries. A big sigh of relief came when the sub surfaced and they were still intact.

Donny was getting bored stiff, so he watched the card games that were going on and learned poker by asking questions. He finally got the nerve up and sat in on a few games. Beginner's luck was not to be with him, and after losing five dollars, he left the game and went back to his bunk and thought of home and Donna. He went up on deck a few times to get away from the tight quarters to just sit up there and watch the fish following them. The sea now was like glass, and more and more shipmates took advantage of the fresh air. A German plane flew overhead, but before anyone panicked, he was gone, never to return. He probably never even saw them was the consensus.

The Germans were being pushed back toward Berlin, with the Americans and Russians all around them. Hitler was now in his underground office, contemplating suicide. He told Eva, whom he had just married, that they couldn't let the Russians capture them alive. "They would put us in a cage for public viewing", he told Eva. A German general, who Hitler had trusted, walked into this office and told Hitler that the plane was ready for him to take them to a chalet in Switzerland. The general told Hitler that the two look-alike people were there, and would be poisoned and then shot as planned. They would then be taken outside and the bodies burned. Everyone, including your own people, will think it's you, my Fuehrer. "Excellent", said Hitler, and he and Eva left by the secret door and were taken by car to the one deserted airstrip on the outskirts of town. The two look-alikes of Eva and Hitler were killed by poison and then shot in the head. The bodies were then carried out in front the bunker and laid in a shallow grave. They were saturated with gasoline and set ablaze. Word spread quickly that Hitler and Eva took their own lives rather than be captured by the Russians. When the Russians came and found the bodies, they were convinced that the two bodies in the shallow grave were that of Hitler and Eva. Even the dental records were fake and reflected that it was them. Stalin was never convinced, but he died and the case was closed.

The plane carrying Hitler and Eva was approaching the Swiss boarder when they hit a storm. The pilot fought the controls to stay airborne. Hitler and Eva were sitting directly behind the pilot's compartment. The co-pilot came to Hitler and told him that they had hit a storm, but should be out of it in a few minutes. "We will go under the storm and start looking for our landing site soon", he said. The plane shuddered now and then, and lightning lit up the skies. Hitler glanced over at Eva, trying not to look scared and said, "We will be at our chalet soon and then, my sweet, we will live like king and queen for the rest of our lives. We have this plane loaded with money and gold". Eva tried her best to smile, but the plane shuddered again, and she turned pale. The pilot went below the storm and saw the small landing site, surrounded by the forest. He maneuvered the plane toward the ground, cutting down his speed, and just as his wheels touched the ground, he saw he was in serious trouble. The ground was soft from all the rain that had fallen all day and the plane skidded and flipped over, hitting the trees in its path, and burst into flames. The last thing Hitler saw were flames engulfing him. His screams could be heard for miles, which sounded like a hurt animal. It was a just ending for a crazed wallpaper hanger. The plane and bodies were never to be found. The snows came and burried the remains forever.

Customers coming to John's store were saying that the war was over, and Germany had surrendered. It wasn't official, but rumors had it that now that Hitler was out of the picture, the new general who took over wanted peace. The United States said that they would accept only an unconditional surrender. Germany had no choice anymore but to take the terms of surrender. American people went wild when the Germans laid down their arms and surrendered. "Steve should be coming home soon", said John.

The Japanese on the other hand weren't ready to lay down their arms. They would fight to the last man if necessary claimed the Japanese emperor.

Chapter XXV

Donny and his unit received another assignment to clear the beach of another Japanese held island in the Pacific so the Marines could land there. Naval intelligence got word that this island was heavily fortified, but had to be taken to shorten the war. This island was close to Japan and, once taken, airports could be built there. They could then bomb the Japanese at will. Plans were in the works to invade Japan, but they estimate close to a million casualties. A battalion of Marines would accompany the Frogmen to keep the Japanese at bay.

The frogmen went back into practicing with high explosives, putting in ten-hour days.

Tom wanted to assure himself that the unit was ready, so he pushed his men to the point of exhaustion. When he felt they were as ready as they ever would be, he told the men to rest until he got the orders to go. Tom didn't have to long to wait. The orders were delivered. That evening Tom got his unit together and told them that they would leave by submarine in the morning. But this time a battalion of marines, whose job would be to knock out the gun emplacements on the beach, would accompany them. Tom told the men to leave their personal items behind, including their dog tags.

Morning came and the trucks were already in front. They loaded and took the short ride to the submarine. Once aboard, they were taken to their compartments and settled in for their trip. Donny got into this bunk and started to think about Donna. Before he left, he wanted to write to her, but with the mission on and all the hours he put in, he just couldn't. They were also under strict orders not to write until they returned. Donny, still tired, closed his eyes and fell asleep.

Steve and his battalion were on the move, clearing out snipers and stragglers who never got word that the war was over. Steve spent a few days riding in a jeep with a German soldier, who was on a loudspeaker informing everyone that the war was over and to lay down their arms. Many German soldiers and officers came forward to surrender. They were quickly searched, and then marched to a holding area set up for the prisoners.

Steve's company was being sent home; they earned it. Steve was going home with three bronze stars for valor. Three days before the war ended, Steve and another member of his squad were sent up on a ridge to observe a bridge that their headquarters believed would be used by retreating German tanks and infantry. They were up on the ridge for two days when they heard the sound of tanks heading for the ridge. They weren't retreating but advancing, with hundreds of fresh troops. Steve called into his command and told them to fire two rounds for effect. The first round sailed thirty yards too long, and so did the second round. Steve yelled, "Thirty yards less", and this time the shell exploded a little too close where they felt the concussion and dirt come on them. "Too short", he screamed into the phone, not caring if the Germans heard him. The next shell was right on target, and hit the lead tank, shells exploding inside the tank. "Right on target", he yelled out.

Steve and the other man tried to get to their feet to run away from the explosions, but were pushed back to the ground. They had to crawl on their bellies for over 200 yards. They finally got up and walked and ran back to their unit. Steve's face was a bloody mess from a cut on his nose, which was quickly attended to by a medic. They took a shower and then made out their report. They were then told to go to sleep. They earned it. The war was over for them.

Final preparations were being made aboard the sub. They were going to submerge soon and stay submerged until they reached their destination tomorrow evening. Donny was getting edgy, and wished they were they there to take his mind off home and Donna. He felt fully prepared and anxious to get going. The worst part of a mission is the waiting. Donny had a restless night and couldn't wait for morning to come. Tom, the leader of the group, told them that this mission would be a piece of cake, just to relax his men. Tom knew that any mission could go wrong, and the enemy could be waiting for them.

The sub surfaced. It was night and the moon was behind the clouds. The Frogmen started to load the boats as the Marines came up on deck with full gear, loading into two boats. Tom told Donny that he and another Frogman named Jim would go directly to the beach to check for any gun emplacements. The Marines would land on the west end and move south toward Tom and Donny, checking for any gun emplacements and troop counts. The balance of the Frogmen would set charges on the obstacles in the water. When they neared the beach, cover was on their side and they slipped over the side.

When Tom, Donny and Jim got to the beach, they found it deserted. They crawled to a hill to get a better look. Tom stopped them as they got near the top and told them to get down. Down below, a handful of Japanese was sitting around a bonfire, enjoying themselves by alighting and talking. Tom didn't see any artillery. Gunfire was heard in the distance. The Marines has stumbled on the Japanese.

The Frogmen setting the charges were finishing up. Now that they had set all the timers, they were ready to leave. When satisfied, the head Frogman of the group verified all the timers were set. He motioned for the unit to swim out to deep water to be picked up by the boats. Tom, Donny and Jim crawled on their stomachs to the top of the hill. They were unaware that a Japanese guard observed them and hid in the brush, waiting for them to come up. The Jap waited until they got to their feet and then opened fire, hitting Jim in the forehead, killing him instantly. Donny jumped to his feet and fired a burst from his gun, hitting the Jap in the chest. The Japanese at the bonfire came to investigate the shooting and were met by hand grenades thrown by Tom and Donny. Donny jumped to his feet and rushed the Japanese, firing his gun in burst after burst. The Japs were falling in piles on top of each other. More Japs came and they were met by rifle fire or grenades thrown. Donny felt a burning sensation in his side, but continued to fire his gun. He only stopped when he saw the Marines come over the hill, shouting and shooting.

Donny went over to meet them and collapsed from his wound. Tom and the Marine captain came to his side and placed a large bandage on his side to stop the bleeding. The captain told Tom that he would take Donny and the dead frogman on the boat to meet the sub. Tom left and swam to meet the other frogmen. The crew of the sub, which was surfaced and waiting for them, helped the Frogmen and the Marines aboard. They carried Donny to sickbay where a medic examined him. The captain was told that Donny needed Surgery to remove the bullets. The captain called to the radioman to see if any ships were close that have surgeons on board. A half-hour later, the radioman told the captain that a carrier was close by with surgeons on board.

The sub surfaced and came alongside the carrier. Donny was transferred to the operating room. Two surgeons worked on him and removed two bullets. They also had to remove his spleen because of the bullets' damage. He was in excellent physical shape and came through the operation well. Tom visited Donny aboard the carrier, as did all of the team. The ship was heading for Norfolk, Virginia. When they arrived in Norfolk, Donny was transferred to a hospital in Portsmouth, where he stayed for three weeks. Donny was healing as well as he could but was told that he no longer could be a Frogman. He may possibly have a limp for the rest of his life.

Tom came in, followed by an admiral, and Donny was presented with the Purple Heart. The admiral told Donny that after two weeks leave, he was to report to Washington, DC to receive the highest award given to a man, the Medal of Honor. He was told that the Vice President would present it to him at a ceremony in his honor. He shook Donny's hand and wished him the best. When the admiral left, Tom stayed in the room and talked to him for over an hour. Donny asked Tom if he would be there with him in Washington, and Tom told him he wouldn't miss it.

Steve's tour of duty was over and he was now on a ship heading for the United States. He was looking forward to civilian life and pictured Barbara in his life. His ship arrived in Norfolk, Virginia, and the Army transported him to an Army base in George, where he was discharged. He called Barbara and asked her to pick him up at the Chicago train station. It seemed like forever on the train, but it finally arrived, and Barbara was there waiting for him as he got off. After fifteen minutes of kissing and hugging, Barbara looked into his tired eyes and said, "Welcome home, sweetheart". Steve asked Barbara if he could drive home. He wanted to marry her as soon as possible. "Is today soon enough", she said with a smile. "Let's start planning our wedding as soon as we get home", he said. "OK", said Barbara. "You're the boss", and shifted her body next to his.

Barbara proceeded to tell Steve about Donny getting wounded and getting the Medal of Honor. "He's supposed to be coming home soon", she said, "and may even be on his way home now". "Oh, that's great news", Steve said. "I sure hope he will be here for our wedding".

Donny was on his way home. He was flying into Midway Airport, and Donna was on her way to pick him up. Donny had a very noticeable limp and was very pale from his days at the hospital. He tried his best to hide the limp as he got off the plane, and headed for the waiting room to meet Donna. She couldn't help but notice it and felt terrible for him. When Donny saw Donna, he wanted to run to her but thought twice when the pain hit him, and he slowed down to a walk. When he got to her, he lifted her up, forgetting the pain for a moment, and then he wept openly. He told Donna how much he missed her, and she wept, saying, "'It's OK, baby, you're home now'. She saw how much he grimaced with paid and said, "Let's get your baggage, honey". Once in the car, Donna drove and she listened. She told Donny that Barbara was on her way to pick up Steve at the train station and he would see him when he got home.

Donna drove Donny to his house, and when they got there John, Mary, Joe and Eleanor were waiting for them on the front stoop. Steve and Barbara were also there with some of the neighbors who heard that both brothers were coming home. Donny, with tears flowing, exited the car slowly with Donna at his side. He was hugged by his mother first, then his Dad and then Steve and Barbara, followed by Joe and El, and last by the neighbors.

The mail came the next morning, and it was an invitation to the White House for Donny's Medal of Honor presentation. Inside were five tickets for the family. Donny asked Steve if he could drive their parents, Barbara and Donna to Washington, DC. "Sure ", he said, "should be fun".

Steve received a letter from the Police Department to report to the Police Academy in two weeks. He received the second highest score in the test he took before being drafted. The Chicago area was in great demand for policemen, and he was a prime candidate for the job. Steve called Barbara to tell her the good news and to tell her about the Washington trip. She told him that she and Donna would love to go, seeing that she never was there and there was so much to see. Barbara now worked as a partner in her father's firm, bringing in a lot of business. Barbara passed her bar exam with a high score, and did well in law school.

It was a nice sunny day when they all left for Washington. They left early to beat the heavy work traffic. They drove for three hours and then stopped for lunch. Barbara called a Howard Johnson motel the day before they left and reserved three rooms for the night. They stooped there and had dinner. On the way they saw this sign that read "Country Music Tonight in the Lounge". Seeing that it still was early and they all enjoyed country music, they went in and stayed there for three hours, then called it a night. They planned to be on the road at 6:00 am. They all had a good night's sleep and met in the restaurant for breakfast. After breakfast, they started out, wide awake, eager to get to their destination. They didn't stop for lunch, but continued on and go to the While House just before noon. They parked the car and were escorted to the Rose Garden.

The Vice President arrived and greeted them all. After a speech that lasted fifteen minutes, he told of Donny's heroic deed, which brought tears to everyone's eyes. He then presented Donny with the Medal of Honor. Tom, the commander of his team, was there. After the ceremony, a steward came in told everyone that refreshments would be served. They made a tour of the White House, which was really impressive. They never thought they would be given such a tour by such an important figure as the Vice President of the United States. They stayed in Washington that evening, taking in all the places that they felt important to see. They headed back the next day, taking their time going home.

Steve went off to the police academy, while Donny's leave had ended and he was to report back to Norfolk, Virginia, for reassignment. The captain of the Frogmen and a commander sat Donny down and asked him if he would ship over for another five years and work at a recruitment center in Chicago. He would be getting first class petty officer rank and nice shipping over bonus. He would be getting a guarantee to remain in Chicago working the hours of 8:00 am to 4:30 pm, with weekends off. Donny thought about it for a moment and figured he would be close to home, and with the bonus he could buy himself a new car. "Where do I sign", he said. He knew this was all due to him receiving the medal. He was told that was soon as the papers are made up, he could leave. "Great", he said. He called his parents and Donna as soon as he had left the office with his papers.

Donny took the train this time. He was in no hurry and needed time to think about the future. The coach was comfortable and the dining car gave him good food. He was surprised that he fell asleep in his chair, and the conductor woke him as they pulled into the Chicago station. Donny took a few minutes to regain his senses and went into the men's room to throw some cold water on his face to wake up. His mouth felt like he had just swallowed his socks. So he kept rinsing his mouth with cold water. He took a piece of gum that he had in his pocket, and that refreshed him some with the cold water on his face. He wasn't 100%, but this would have to do.

Barbara called Steve at the academy to tell him about Donny's good fortune, working downtown. Donna got to the train station a few minutes before the train pulled in, and sat down in the waiting room, all excited, knowing that Donny would be home for good. Donna saw him first and called out to him. He was still bothered by his bad leg and was told to use a cane for better balance. But he was too vain for that and left the cane on the train. They embraced when they met, and Donny told her that he had to report to his new job at the recruiting station downtown in one week. He was excited about it and felt like a civilian again.

The week flew by, but he still had the time to go with Uncle Joe to buy a new car, which he felt he deserved after putting his signature on a contract for five more years. Donny was getting dressed, putting on his tailor-made dress whites for his first day on the job. He wondered what his first day would be. He was putting on weight since he got home, and thought he'd better start exercising soon. Donny thought he would get up a half-hour earlier each morning, starting next week, and start his calisthenics and walk a mile in the evening. He was told that a parking spot would be reserved for him in case he wanted to drive to work. Today, his first day, he would take the bus and then the El, which would take him a block from the recruitment center.

He caught the bus a block from home, and as he went to pay his fare, the bus driver said "No charge for servicemen". He then asked Donny, "Aren't you the Medal of Honor winner"? "Yes, said Donny, and then shook the outstretched hand of the driver. The bus took Donny to Logan Square, where he got off and walked a short distance to the El. He went up the stairs, and caught the El train in a few minutes. The ride took about a half-hour. He got off and headed for the stairs. As he descended the stairs and got to the bottom step, he was met by a young man, a knife in his right hand.

He told Donny to give him his wallet or he will stab him. He kept flashing the knife back and forth, trying to scare Donny. Today he picked on the wrong person to rob, because Donny was an expert in hand-to-hand combat.

The thief was getting impatient and went to lunge at Donny, but Donny grabbed the man's arm, twisted it until he heard the snap of the bone. The thief screamed bloody murder. Donny gave him a karate chop that silenced him and he went down to his knees. A police officer, walking his beat across the street, witnessed the attempted robbery and came running over with gun drawn. "Are you OK?" asked the officer. "I'm fine but I don't think he is", pointing to the thief. The officer called for an ambulance and then took down Donny's report of the incident.

Chapter XXVI

A reporter came by and took down all the facts. The ambulance arrived, and the thief was taken away to the hospital. Donny was told that he could leave then, and went to the office. He got there late, but after explaining to the chief what he encountered, the chief felt bad about Donny's first day at his new job. The office closed for lunch at noon, and the chief took Donny out to lunch.

When Donny got home from his first day, his Mom made him his favorite meal, stuffed cabbage. He told his parents about his incident and said that his picture may be in the paper tomorrow morning. "Like father, like son", Said Mary, recalling the time John hit the thief with a hot iron and sent him to the hospital. "Are you OK", asked Mary? "Fine", said Donny, "not a scratch". When the paper arrived in the morning, the article and Donny's picture were on page two: "Medal of Honor winner; hero again"!

Steve was doing well at the academy and had no trouble making the grades. They planned on getting married after Steve's graduation. They were now in the process of looking for an apartment, which they found four doors from her Dad's office. Steve was very happy about it because he didn't want Barbara driving to work in the cold, icy winters that Chicago has. The landlord was a very good friend of Barbara's parents and told them about the apartment being empty soon. They rushed over there and looked at the apartment, which was in excellent condition and was on the second floor. It had two bedrooms, an eat-in kitchen, with a large living room. They took it.

Steve's graduation came, and both families were there. He came in third in his class, and was now a Chicago police officer. When Steve got home, they went to buy some paint and brushes, and then headed for the apartment. Barbara wanted to have the bedrooms painted before showing the apartment off. Steve could have waited until after they moved in and settled, but wanted to keep peace and went along with her. Barbara's father volunteered to help, as did Donny, but Barbara thanked them and said it's only the bedrooms that needed paint. So the two of them went right at it and finished the next day, working until midnight.

Steve was happy that he didn't have to start his job for two weeks, which gave them time to get married and go for a week on their honeymoon. The new priest that took over Father Joe's job would marry the couple. It was going to be a small wedding, less than seventy people coming to the reception. All the inviting was done by phone. Steve's family was small. Most of the guests that were coming were on Barbara's side. The reception was to be held at a restaurant close to home. The owner of the restaurant was a big client of Frank's and would bend backwards for them. Donna would be the maid of honor, while Donny would be the best man. After the reception, they would fly to Bermuda, on Grotto Bay, for four days.

John, Joe, Steve and Donny headed for the tux shop along with Frank, who was a friend of the owner. The owner took care of the whole party and guaranteed that the tuxes would be ready before the wedding. They were all told to come in two days before the wedding to try on the tuxes in case alterations had to be made.

The big day arrived and Barbara looked beautiful, and Steve as handsome as ever. Frank walked Barbara to the altar with a tear in his eye, knowing he would have to repeat this again soon with Donna. Steve met them at the altar entrance and was smiling. Frank lifted Barbara's veil and gave his daughter a kiss, saying, "I love you, my little one". Then he turned to face Steve and shook his hand. The new priest, whose name was Father Bo (short for his last name, Bonack) got Steve and Barbara to the center of the altar and said, "You two make a lovely couple". They recited their vows and Father Bo gave Barbara a kiss on the cheek and shook Steve's hand. He said, "Good luck to you both and go now with God's blessing".

Everyone now was heading for the reception. Father Bo told them he would meet them at the reception for a prayer. The bride, groom, parents and Busia went to a park for picture taking. The roses in the park and the other plants were in full bloom, and the colors were fantastic for picture taking. This took an hour, and they then headed for the reception, which was then in full swing. The restaurant supplied the band, and they played their favorite music, which most people enjoyed. The dance floor was always packed. The wedding lasted until midnight and then Steve and Barbara left, letting, Donna, Donny and their parents know. They left for a motel for the night. They planned to catch a flight to Bermuda at 9:00 am. They had their suitcases all packed, ready to go. Donny and Donna were to pick them up at 7:00 am to take them to the airport.

Barbara was the first to get up. She glanced over at Steve, who was starting to stir. She bent over him and planted a kiss on him and said, "Good morning, husband of mine". With that, he sat up. "Good morning, sweet wife of mine. What time is it, honey"? "5:30 am", she said. Time for a shower and coffee before Donna and Donny get here. While you're in the shower, I'll call the airport and confirm our flight". "OK", he grunted, and left the room. They were having breakfast in the restaurant when Donna and Donny walked in and said, "Are we early"? "Have a cup of coffee you two and then we can go", said Steve, anxious to get started. Donny drove and found traffic light "How does it feel, being married", asked Donny with a grin on his face. "Stop it", said Barbara, "and drive the car". They got to the airport 45 minutes before the flight's departure and sat in the waiting room, talking. Their flight was finally called. "See you guys when we get back", said Steve, "and don't forget to be here when we get back". "Don't worry, you two", said Donna. "I have it written down". "Good", said Steve, "Just don't forget where you wrote it down". Donny and Donna waited until the plane was airborne before they left.

The flight was nice and smooth, and even lunch was served on the short flight. When they arrived in Bermuda, a limo was on hand to take them to the hotel. A clerk met them as they departed the limo, and took their luggage to their room. All the rushing around they did prior to their wedding caught up to them and they just collapsed on the bed and fell asleep in each other's arms.

When they awoke from their nap, they were refreshed and started to unpack. They had glass sliding doors leading to the beach. A table and two chairs were also out there. A bottle of wine and a basket of fruit were in the room, compliments of the hotel. Barbara was looking out the glass doors and said, "Let's go take those putt boats out there before we go to dinner". "OK", said Steve. They put on their bathing suits and headed to the dock. The sun was hot and they wanted to get a tan, but didn't realize how hot it was. They paddled for over an hour, taking in the beautiful sights. When they returned to the dock, the owner of the boats mentioned their sunburn, but then they didn't feel it. After dinner, the sunburn was taking its toll, so they took a ride into town by bus and bought a large jar of

Noxzema. They loaded themselves down with the cream and went outside and sat in the chairs, catching some of the ocean breezes. They had trouble sleeping because of the sunburn, and used up all of the Noxzema. After breakfast they headed back into town to pick up more Noxzema. They were both hurting and looked like two red apples. "Let's stay out of the sun today", said Barbara. "I agree", said Steve.

Back home, Donny was getting adjusted to his recruiting job and enjoying it. He had been taking the bus and El to work every day. He felt it was the most economical way to go. Traffic was always heavy in the mornings, and twice as bad trying to get home. He only drove when he had a meeting out of town. Those days he dreaded.

He proposed to Donna while Steve and Barbara were in Bermuda. They went together to buy the ring and set their wedding date in two months. They couldn't wait to tell Barbara and Steve.

Steve and Barbara met a couple at dinner who they teamed up with and started going places with them. Their names were Marion and Dan. They lived in the suburbs of New York and were celebrating their fifth wedding anniversary. Marion was a secretary for a lawyer group, and Dan was a dentist in his early forties. The four of them got along great. One day they took out motor scooters and spent the day looking at the farmlands and beautiful flowers. They brought sandwiches and drinks with them and sat on the side of the road, having a picnic and talking. Steve and Dan noticed that they didn't see any gas stations around, so they thought it best to call it a day and head back before they ran out of gas and had to push the scooters back. They got back in time for dinner, and all four of them were tanned.

After dinner, they took a walk to an underground disco. When they walked in, the dank smell hit them. There was water on both sides of the catwalk, and then they got to the dance floor, which was empty. A few couples were sitting around the bandstand. The band was loud, and after having one drink, they danced for a half-hour and decided to leave. It was good to breathe the fresh air outside. They took a walk to the ice cream parlor on the corner, and talked about their families and made plans to take the bus into town in the morning.

The next morning they met for breakfast and then took the bus into town. Barbara wanted to buy tee shirts with the Bermuda logo on them for everyone in the family. Marion and Dan came from a large family, and the buying started with the first store advertising shirts. Steve and Dan stood in one corner talking, not getting in the girls' way. Every now and then, the girls would bring a shirt over to show them, and they would nod their approval.

With their shopping bags full, the wives were ready for lunch. They found a nice little restaurant in the center of town and went in, ordering a pizza for themselves. The men ordered a beer, which they deserved for not getting in the way while the girls shopped. After a light lunch of pizza, they left and visited and old schooner, of which they took a roll of film. Steve and Barbara didn't want their honeymoon to end. "Back to work on Monday", Barbara said. "Yes", said Steve, "all good things must come to an end".

Donna and Donny took a ride to the church they planned to get married in and asked for Father Bok who was available and welcomed them into his office. After listening to them, he pulled out a calendar and told them the date would be fine. The next stop was the restaurant where Steve and Barbara had their reception. They enjoyed the food, the band and the place itself at Barbara's and Steve's wedding, and they wanted their reception there. The manager told them the date was open, so they put down a deposit to hold it for them. The owner told them to stop over next week to pick out the menu. The restaurant would furnish the band, and they would have to furnish them a list of any special songs they wanted to hear. "I can't wait to tell Barbara", Donna said. "Well, you won't have to wait too long', Donny said. "They will be home next week".

Marion and Dan were staying for three more days, and told Steve and Barbara that they had such a great time with them and that they wished they could stay another few days. "I wish we could, but work calls, and all good things must come to an end", said Steve. "We sure will miss you guys", said Barbara, "But I will write you once we get settled in". "Good", said Marion. "Let's keep in touch by writing each other once a month. Maybe in a year or so we can plan on meeting each other here for a vacation". "Sounds super", said Barbara.

"We will see you guys off on Monday, but tonight how about taking a taxi into town. I heard that Frankie Avalon is playing in one of the hotels. We can buy the tickets at our motel. I saw it advertised this morning". "OK", they said, and headed for the office. That evening after dinner, they got a cab and headed for the hotel. The cab driver was in a hurry and must have been an auto racer, because he turned corners at high speed, squealing tires, probably trying to impress them with his driving. Steve told him to slow down, as did Dan, but it didn't do any good. They got to the hotel in one piece, but were rattled by his driving. The show was outstanding, and they enjoyed themselves. Frankie Avalon went from table to table, serenading all the women. The ride back to the motel was the same, but they finally got back and had a drink at the bar before turning in.

Frank and Rose had been helping Donna call all the relatives and friends to invite them to their daughter's wedding. They didn't realize how many friends they had, plus clients that had become friends. The total figure was higher than Barbara's wedding by ten. They were asked by Donna to go with them to the restaurant to make the arrangements. "Boy", said Frank, "Who would ever think we would be having both of our daughters getting married in one year"? "Yes", said Rose, "isn't it great"?

Donna and Donny were on their way to the airport to pick up Steve and Barbara, all excited to tell them about their wedding plans. Donna just started her new job at the bank close to home. She would get two weeks off for her wedding. She was a very good accountant. They were lucky to find a house for sale directly across the street from Barbara and Steve's apartment. Donny had some money left over from his re-enlistment plus the money he had been putting aside in the bank for his occasion. They could put down a good-sized down payment. By renting the two apartments over theirs, they could pay off the house quickly.

The plane was on schedule, and walking off the plane was a happy and tanned couple. After hugging, they went to pick up the luggage and then headed for the car. "We have a surprise for you guys", Donna said. She couldn't hold it back any longer. "We're getting married in two weeks, and bought a house directly opposite your apartment". "Where do you plan on going for your honeymoon", asked Steve. "Well", said Donny, "maybe we'll go to Lake Geneva or the Poconos". They made their decision about the honeymoon by thinking of a 24-hour drive to the Poconos versus a two-hour trip to Lake Geneva. They both agreed on Lake Geneva, which would give them time to come home and get into the painting.

Donna and Donny's wedding day arrived, and the photographer was at their house early in the morning, taking pictures of her preparing for their big day. Barbara and her Mom were right there pitching in to get her ready. Donny, on the other hand, was a nervous wreck, pacing back and forth and asking for the time so that they could leave for the church. He had his tux on, as did Steve and his father. The men looked handsome, and Mary looked beautiful in her violet dress. "Why does the time drag", asked Donny. "Patience, brother", said Steve. "It will be here and gone before you know it. Now relax and stop looking at the clock". "I can't help it", he said. "Maybe I should call Donna'. "No way; you don't see her or talk to her", said Steve. Uncle Joe came down, all dressed in his tux. "How is Donny holding up", he asked? "He's a nervous wreck", said Steve.

"OK", yelled Steve. "Time to go". Steve drove Donny's car. It was newer and shines up. The church was only minutes away, and when they got there, they saw Frank pulling up in front. They hurried Donny into the church so he wouldn't see Donna. Steve and Donny were at the steps leading to the altar when the music started. Frank started to walk his daughter down the aisle. She looked beautiful coming down the aisle. When they got in front of the altar, Frank kissed his daughter and gave her to Donny, who was all smiles. Father Bo was waiting for them at the altar. They approached the priest, and after taking their vows, they both turned and started out. Donny was all smiles now.

The reception was nice, but went too fast, they both thought. Donna and Donny left the reception while the band played a slow dance, and most of the guests were dancing. They went to a motel for the night, and were up early, ate breakfast as husband and wife, and headed out for Lake Geneva. Just before they left, Donna made a call to Barbara and invited her and Steve to come and visit them at Lake Geneva at the end of the week before they were to come home.

Mary and John received word from the Red Cross that her sister, Jen, and brother-in-law, Ted, were alive and well and live not far from where they once lived. Mary wrote to them and asked them to come to America. Mary and John bought a three-story home and told her sister that they could have the apartment above them. Mary was very happy now, and when Mary was happy, so was he.

Chapter XXVII

When Donna and Donny arrived at Lake Geneva, the line was long for registration, but they were in no hurry and got in line. They began talking to a couple in front of them, a couple from New York, Bob and Blanche. They were celebrating their 25th wedding anniversary. Bob was a truck driver, delivering material from state to state. Blanche worked in a library and enjoyed her job, being there for twelve years. Donna and Donny spent a lot of time with them, going to nightclubs in the evening. Dancing usually followed the show, and Donny surprised Donna by dancing a lot and enjoying it.

Barbara went to the doctor to verify that she was pregnant. It was no surprise when she was told that she is pregnant. Steve was hoping for a little Stevie.

Mary and John got the ball rolling to get her sister, Jen, to America. Money was sent and received by Jenny and Ted. Their ship was due to leave for America in three weeks. Preparations to have the apartment ready for them were started, and Mary was in her glory. John was happy to see her this excited and keeping busy.

Barbara called Lake Geneva and left a message for Donna that they would come to spend Friday with them. They met them in front of their cottage Friday at noon and spent the full day showing them around. Dinner was on them, and in the evening they invited Bob and Blanche to go to a club with them. They had a great time and hated to see Barbara and Steve go home.

The following morning they were all packed and ready to make the trip home. They said their good-byes to Bob and Blanche and promised to write each other. They were happy now that they had chosen this place, having only a two-hour trip home.

Steve's first day on the job was very boring. He met his partner, Ron Zaine, who had five years on the force. He was six feet tall, weighing in at 200 pounds plus. He would be the one you would want on your side in case of any confrontation with the bad guys. Ron lived two miles from Steve, was married and the father of two boys. He drove the squad car and gave Steve tips on being a cop. They received a few calls, mostly wives arguing with husbands, a street fight, and a drunk not wanting to leave a bar.

After three days of this, they got a call of a shooting in a bar. They responded with sirens blaring and were there in two minutes. As they entered the bar, Ron told him to follow his lead and to watch his back. They noticed a man sitting at the end of the bar with a pistol in his hand. Two patrons were on the floor moaning. "OK", said Ron to the man, "slide the gun across the bar to me. You did enough damage for one day". The man just looked at him and smiled. Steve drew his gun, bent down on one knee, and pointed the gun right at the man. The man looked in Steve's direction and saw the barrel of the gun pointed directly at him. "Slide the gun across the bar", yelled Steve. The man slowly moved his arm with the gun in it toward the bar and cried out, "OK, don't shoot". He then slid the gun across the bar to Ron. Steve holstered his gun and then came forward to the man and put the man's hands behind his back and put handcuffs on him. "Good job", said Ron.

Ron went over and checked on the two patrons lying on the floor. He saw that their wounds weren't life threatening. He did what he could for them, and then waited for the ambulance to come. When the ambulance came, the two men shot were taken to the hospital, treated and then released. The handcuffed man was taken into the wagon and was taken to a cell. He stayed in jail for a long time. Ron complimented Steve on a good job, which made him feel good.

Steve was happy that he earned Ron's respect. After that day, Steve and Ron became close friends. They started going to each other's homes and double dated.

Steve and Ron got along real good. Barbara at times felt a little jealous and knew it was silly of her to feel that way. When the two of them were together, they constantly talked police business and enjoyed each other's company. After all, they spent all week together, and sometimes even on Saturday if they pulled a work detail.

Barbara did have Steve on Sunday, even though the day was spent listening to football games or resting, or even some days visiting his parents. "Things will get better", she thought.

Steve loved being a cop and he was good at it, especially enjoying helping people whenever he could.

Chapter XXVIII

One day, while on patrol on State Street, Ron stopped at a deli and told Steve he was going into the deli for a sandwich and coffee and asked Steve if he wanted anything. Steve always had a sandwich made by Barbara the night before, and always with a note inside which read "I love you and be careful, my love". He enjoyed the notes. Steve asked Ron to get him a soda and offered him some money, which Ron refused, saying it's on him. Steve noticed a patrol car near the deli, which Rob walked over to. The two cops shook hands and Steve noticed the officer handing a white envelope to Ron, which he tucked into this back pocket. Ron gave the officer a quick salute and went into the deli.

After a few minutes, Ron came back to the car carrying a brown paper bag. As he got into the car, he handed Steve a bottle of soda, saying, "Here you are, partner". Steve thanked him and they were on their way. After having any easy morning and light afternoon, it was getting down to quitting time and time to head back to the station house. A few blocks from the station, Ron pulled into a parking lot, parked the car and turned off the ignition. He reached into his back pocket and brought out the envelope. He opened it in front of Steve and Steve's mouth flew open, seeing a stack of 20's in the envelope. "Wow", he said. "Not bad for a day's work, huh Steve"? "Half of this is yours", said Ron. He counted out twenty 20's and handed it to Steve, saying, "It is found money, tax deferred, Steve. You will get your share each month". Steve, dumbfounded, cried out "I can't take the money, Ron. It's not right". "Take it", Ron said. We all do it. It's OK". "No", said Steve, "I can't". "Look", said Ron. "Take it and do whatever you want with it. Give it to charity or whatever. You can't refuse while you are my partner. You can always use the extra money". Steve didn't know what to do, so he put it in his pocket. He would ask Barbara what he should do. "Thanks", said Steve. "OK now", said Ron. "You had me a little concerned. We are brothers, you know, and brothers help one another". Steve thought that he really laid it on thick.

They stopped talking after that, and after signing out at the station they headed for home. When they pulled into Steve's driveway, Ron said "Good night", and Steve went into this house.

Chapter XXIX

Barbara has always tried to meet Steve as he comes in the door. She felt it was a good habit to get into. Today, as she met him at the door, she saw a sad face on Steve and questioned him. "What's wrong, Steve", she said. "Bad day?" "No worse that that. Barb, let's sit down and I will tell you". "Wow", she said "That bad?" Before he even sat down, Steve no longer could hold it back. "Ron gave me money, payoff money. I didn't want to take it, but he kept insisting, so I put it in my pocket. It is payoff money, Barb. I only took it to keep from starting trouble with him. I don't want this kind of money. I only want to be a good copy". Barbara looked at him and didn't know what to say. "I'm sorry, Steve. Can't you just refuse it? "I tried", Steve said, "but he wouldn't have it like that. He forced me to take it. Said we were partners." "Why don't you put the money in an envelope and let me talk to my Dad about this. He may know what to do". "OK, Barb. I guess that's about the best advice for the time being".

Steve had a miserable night's sleep. He tossed and turned all night, waking Barbara in doing so. She, too, had a bad night.

Steve got up early, showered, shaved and got dressed. Barbara got up before Steve did and had breakfast ready on the kitchen table when he walked in. Steve ate, talked briefly to Barb and got ready to go out the door. "Have a good safe day, honey", said Barbara. "OK", said Steve. "Love you Barb". They kissed and Steve went out on the driveway, waiting for Ron who came on schedule. Steve got into the car and said, "Good morning, Ron". "Morning, Steve", was Ron's reply. Ron was talkative, as usual. "What do we have to do to get those Cubbies motivated"? "Yeah", said Steve. "The pitching is bad., Have to bring up some good ones from the minors or spend some of that money to buy some good pitchers like the Yankees do". It was good that they talked sports instead of the job and the money. The day went quickly by, with no problems.

Chapter XXX

Barbara met Steve at the front door, hoping Steve was in a better mood. He was, giving Barbara a big kiss, hug and half carrying her inside the house. Barbara and Steve had dinner and then she said that she spoke to her Dad, and he suggested that Steve talk to Internal Affairs, a watchdog in the police department. He told her he would look into it.

A few weeks passed and Ron and Steve continued their daily patrol, never mentioning the money. At times Ron would tell Steve that he could use a new car, but that was all.

Steve started to inquire about the Internal Affairs and their function, being very coy about it. He got to know the building they were in and told himself that he would stop in and see them soon. He didn't want to hurt Ron or have him hear that he went to see them. It would have to be when Ron was off or away for the day.

One day when Ron called in sick, Steve made up his mind to pay Internal Affairs a visit. It was lunchtime and Steve, catching up on paperwork since Ron was out, went to the Office of Internal Affairs. He walked in and was approached by a receptionist, asking who he wanted to see. Steve told her that he would like to talk to someone in authority, but can't be seen talking to him. She said that she understood and told him she would get someone. A few minutes passed and then she returned with a big, balding man in his 50's. He introduced himself to Steve, saying his name is Vincent Blake. He asked Steve to follow him to a back room in the office. "You are safe to talk here", he said. "Feel free to tell me what is on your mind". Steve felt very nervous and felt the perspiration on his forehead. He told Vincent his name, badge number and department. He told Vincent that he was given $400.00 by his partner. He said he was pressured into taking it and put it in an envelope for safekeeping. Vincent thanked him and said he wished more cops were willing to come forward and try to do their job that they were hired to do. He told Steve to continue working with Ron as usual. They shook hands and Vincent told Steve to be patient and he will hear from him soon.

When Steve left, he felt like he did something wrong. "I hope Ron never gets word of this", he thought. He told Barbara of his visit with Vincent, and she was glad he went.

Months went by with no word from Vincent. Steve felt like his meeting with Vincent was forgotten about.

One morning Steve went to get the daily paper lying on his driveway and found an envelope attached to the paper. He opened it when he got in the house and found a message from Vincent. The message read, "Meet me at the Greasy Spoon on Hamlin and Springston Street at 2:00 p.m.", and it was signed "V". Steve knew of the place. He ate there once or twice. It was a hangout for young kids. He got there at 1:45 p.m., looked around, saw nobody outside, so he went inside. He saw Vincent sitting at a back table near the wall. Steve sat down opposite Vincent without speaking or looking directly at him. The waitress came to the table and gave Steve a menu. He looked at her and told her "thank you, but I just want a hamburger and coke". Vincent ordered the same and waited for the waitress to leave before speaking to Steve. "Hi", he said. "I'm sorry I haven't contacted you sooner, but I had to do some checking and groundwork on Ron". "That's OK", said Steve. "We are planning to bust up this ring. We knew of the top honchos involved. It's a protection racket started by a detective. I won't tell you his name because the less you know the better it will be for you". "I understand", said Steve. "it is a multi-million dollar racket, and involves top brass. I want you to continue to play their game. Once we spring the trap, many arrests will be made. You may be implicated, but will be transferred to cover yourself". "OK", said Steve as they said their good-byes. Steve went home feeling pretty good now. On the way home, he thought, "What would happen to Ron. Would he go to jail?"

Chapter XXXI

When he got home, Barbara was still at her Dad's office, so he sat on the couch, put on the TV and started to watch the Cubbies. He soon fell asleep and was awakened by a kiss from Barbara. "Hi, honey", he said. "I guess I dozed off". "I guess you did, hon; how was your day"? He told Barbara about the meeting with Vincent. "Good", Barbara said. "When is all this going to take place"? "I don't know, babe, but it will soon".

It was Steve's turn to drive, so he went to pick up Ron. He didn't see Ron in the driveway as he pulled in. He blew his horn, figuring Ron was running late, which he seldom does. He blew his horn again, and then saw the front door opening. Ron's wife, Emma, came out in her bathrobe. "Steve", she cried out, "something has happened. The police came and took Ron away in handcuffs. What's going on"? "I don't know", said Steve, "But I'll call you when I find out". When Steve got to the station, the place was in an uproar. Everyone was talking about the big bust.

The desk sergeant told Steve that a big shakeup is going on with top brass being arrested. Steve tried to play it cool, asking the questions. Steve was assigned a new partner what was much older than Steve and was transferred to another division. His new partner drove the patrol car, which was fine with Steve. His name was Tom and he was a sergeant. Neither one wanted to discuss the shakeup, it was OK with Steve. They had a slow day with the neighborhood being peaceful for once. Lunch was brief and they just talked about their families. Tom was married with two children, looking forward to ten more years so he could retire. When they returned to the station, Steve was called into a meeting with the rest of the division. They were told that more arrests will follow, but to continue doing their duties.

Ron was released on bail pending investigation. He was suspended without pay until the hearing. Steve got a call from Ron that evening which surprised him. "Hi, Steve", said Ron. "What do you hear?" "Hi, Ron. What happened? The station is in an uproar. It is over?" "No", said Ron. "I'm suspended awaiting trail. Keep you ears opened, Steve, and let me know if you hear anything, OK?" "Sure thing, Ron", said Steve. "I'll keep in touch".

Chapter XXXII

When Steve got home he told Barbara that he was not sure if he wanted to continue as a cop. Barbara told him that whatever his decision was, she will back him up. "You know what you will be up against, so don't worry about us. I know we can get along. I will go into practice with my Dad and bring in more money, and whatever you want to do you can bring in the rest. OK Steve"? He took Barbara in his arms and said, "You have enough to do around here with the house, and soon the second baby will come. You have your hands full. Besides, I don't want you to work". "OK, Steve, let's just drop it for now".

Steve didn't sleep very well that night. He tossed and turned and waited for daylight so he could get up and get the day over with. Finally, the light came through and Steve actually jumped out of bed and headed for the shower. Barbara had breakfast ready for Steve and he ate in silence. When he was dressed and ready to go out the door, Barbara gave him a kiss and a hug and wished him a good day. "Thanks honey. I'll see you later".

He got in his car and his mind drifted to the times he and Ron drove in together. It seemed like a long ride to the station. When he drove in with Ron, time passed quickly because they would talk about the Bears and the Cubs. When he turned into the parking lot, he found a spot open close to the door of the station. Steve's heart started to pound as he got out of his car and headed for the door. He walked over to the Sergeants' desk and told the Sergeant he was here to report to work. The Sergeant told him that they expected him and told him to report to the Captain's room.

Steve knocked on the door of the Captain's room and was told to go in. The Captain was sitting at his desk and welcomed Steve. He shook Steve' hand and introduced himself as Captain Frank Martin. He told Steve to relax while he made a phone call. Steve heard Martin say, "Send in Richard Degan". A few minutes later, the door opened and a huge man walked in. Steve estimated him at 6"4", weighing in at 240 lbs. The Captain brought over Richard and introduced him to Steve. They shook hands and Steve was told that Richard was an eight-year patrolman, has two division citation, one for disarming a knife wielding man and was involved in stopping a holdup at a gas station. He told Steve and Richard to sit in the cafeteria and get acquainted. "Tomorrow you'll begin your partnership", said the Captain.

When Steve got home, he told Barbara that everything went well. He was introduced to his new partner, a nice guy, family man, who seems to be a good honest cop. He will drive the patrol car, since he has the seniority and said he would like to drive. He lives about ten miles from here, and for the time being we will drive alone. Maybe when we get to know each other we can carpool. "I guess you will stay a cop", said Barbara. "Yeah", said Steve. "It looks that way".

Donny and Donna stopped over after dinner, and they played canasta. Steve told Donny about his new partner and Donny mentioned how relaxed he finally looked. "It took a lot out of me", said Steve, meaning his problem with Ron. "Yeah", said Donny, "I can see how it would". They had coffee and cake after the card game and called it an early night. When Donny and Donna were going out the door, Donny turned to Steve and said, "I'm really happy for you, Steve". "Thanks", said Steve. "It really means a lot to hear that".

Steve helped Barbara clean up and said he was going to get ready for bed. "I have a long day tomorrow with my new partner". "OK", said Barbara. "Go ahead. I'll finish up". Steve got a good night's sleep, the first in many days.

While Barbara was cleaning up, she was smiling now, felling really good that Steve is back to his old self again.

Chapter XXXIII

Steve drove to the station house, anxious to start the day. He signed in and he and Richard were briefed, as was the rest of the squad. Steve automatically got in the passenger side and Richard in the driver seat. They had their route mapped out and Richard drove off. It was a slow morning, but neither one minded. They stopped for lunch at a small diner, ate a hamburger and a coke and went back to patrolling the streets.

About 2:00 in the afternoon, they got a call about a man on a bridge; looked like a possible suicide and to check it out. When they got to the bridge, they got out of the car and went to check it out. No one was on the bridge that they could see. They looked in the water and spotted a person flailing their arms as if in trouble. Steve took his shoes off, along with his belt and gun and jumped into the water, Richard doing the same. They reached the person who turned out to be a woman in her 30's. She told Steve to stay away and let her drown. "No way", said Steve, who dove into the water and came up behind her. He put his arms around her and Richard, seeing that Steve had her in control, moved in to help him. The woman struggled, but was helpless with the two men holding her up and swimming to shore. When they got the woman to shore, Steve and Richard carried her to dry land. Richard got his handcuffs and handcuffed the woman so she would stay put. Steve went back on the bridge, got his and Richard's shoes, belt and gun and returned to Richard, who was talking to the woman. Steve and Richard were soaked but managed to put on their shoes, belt and gun and walked the woman to the squad car. They rode to the station to make out their report.

When they go to the station, they turned the woman over to detectives. The Sergeant at the desk tried to joke about their condition. "Enjoy your swim, boys?" The look they gave the Sergeant gave him their answer. His smile disappeared.

Steve and Richard went to the locker room, took a shower, put on clean, dry clothes and went to make out their report. Their tour was done for the day, so Steve left, got into his car and went home. Barbara met Steve at the door and asked him how his day was. He told Barbara about the woman in the water and how the two of them jumped into the water to save her.

Chapter XXXIV

Rose was having headaches that bothered her and kept her from sleeping. She told Frank that she will have to go to the doctor if the headaches don't go away. Rose was spending a lot of time dozing on the couch, and Frank was getting worried. She was a strong woman, he thought. These headaches must really be bad to lay her up like this. The headaches continued until she no longer could put up with them. She called the doctor and made an appointment to see him in a couple of days.

She hadn't seen a doctor for a few years, so she was a little nervous when she finally went. She explained her headaches to the doctor and upon examining her, he told her that he felt she had a sinus problem. He gave her a prescription and told her that the medication should get rid of the headaches. After she finished the medication, the doctor told her to come back, so upon leaving she made an appointment in two weeks. On the way home, Rose stopped at a druggist and had her prescription filled and then went home. Frank asked her how she did at the doctor's and wanted to know what the doctor said. She told him the doctor felt it was a sinus problem and gave her pills to take. She hoped the pills would help get rid of the headaches.

Steve and Richard were having slow, easy days patrolling the streets of Chicago. The woman who jumped off the bridge was the most exciting event in weeks. They didn't mind the slow and boring days. They knew they would face a robbery or a shooting soon. They didn't have long to wait. That afternoon they got a call of a shooting. A jewelery store was being robbed not far from where they were. Richard put his foot down on the acclerator and, tires screeching, they sped to the scene of the shooting. They were at the jewelry store in minutes, hitting the brakes in the front with guns drawn, and going on foot to the store. They were met by the owner in front of the store, who told them that the robbers had run off on foot in the west direction. Steve and Richard gave chase in that direction, after Richard got on the radion to inform the station that they were in pursuit of the two robbers. They ran to the end of the block and came to a section of brush there and a huge amount of shrubbery. "A good place to hide", said Steve. "Yeah", said Richard. "I'm sure they're in there. Be extra careful". "Maybe we should wait for help", said Steve. "I got the call in and I'm sure the cavalry will arrive soon". Just then two squad cars came into view with three more behind them. Richard met the other officers and told them that he thought the thieves were hiding in the brush. "They're armed", he said.

A sergeant arrived to join the group and took over the command. He led four officers to go to one corner of the woods and when he gave the signal, to start walking in, heading North. Another four officers would enter from the right and watch for movement. The sergeant sent one of the patrolmen for a megaphone. When he returned, the sergeant called out for the thieves to come out with their hands over their heads. A shot rang out and almost hit the sergeant. All the officers standing around hit the dirt. No one was hit, but they didn't see where the shot came from. The sergeant gave the orders to move into the woods. Steve and Richard went in from the front. After taking a few steps forward, two shots rang out grazing Richard in the forearm. Steve hit the dirt and saw two figures in the brush. He fired off two rounds in the direction of the two men. He checked on Richard who said he was OK. "Just a nick", he said. Steve saw the four officers who came in from the left and they started to fire their rifles in the thieves' direction. Steve heard one thief yell out that he was hit and to stop firing. Steve went forward, very cautiously, and pointed his gun in front of him. The other four officers on his left got to the thief before he did. When he got there, the officers were handcuffing him. He then looked down and saw the other thief with a bullet wound to the chest. He was dead.

Their shift was ending, so they went back to the starion, made out their report, and called it a day. Steve mentioned the shooting to Barbara, but didn't really go into the shooting that much. He didn't even menition Richard getting shot or nicked. It would only upset Barbara. He ate, watched a little TV and called it a night. He told Barbara that he walked a lot and was tired. She looked as if she understood and said, "Good night, Steve. I love you".

Chapter XXXV

The next day at the station all you could hear was the robbery and shooting. Richard had his nick looked at by a doctor and was bandaged, and that was that.

He and Richard were interviewed by detectives and gave their story; then the morning was almost over. They spent the afternoon cruising the streets without one call. Richard asked Steve to come over to his house with Barbara on Saturday. He said he would call Barbara from the station to make sure they were free. "Fine", said Richard. Richard was eight years older than Steve, but he didn't look it. He still had that boyish look about him. Steve called Barbara from the station and asked her if they could go to Richard's home on Saturday for a get-together. "No problem", said Barbara. It would be nice to meet Richard's wife.

Steve told Richard that he never mentioned him getting nicked by the bullet to Barbara, and told him why he didn't. "I understand", said Richard. "I won't bring it up, I promise".

The rest of the week was very quiet for Steve and Richard. They had two small gang fights, a family disturbance where they took the husband to the station for hitting his wife. Before they booked him, a call came in from the wife who said that she won't press charges. It was a mistake. They released the husband and got him a ride home. They told him that they had better not get anymore calls about him beating his wife, because it will be jail time for him. They both felt that they scared him enough to think twice before hitting her.

Saturday came and Steve and Barbara drove to Richard's house on the outskirts of Des Plaines. They found the place with no problem. It was a nice Cape Cod. The lawn was nicely manicured and thick. On the way there, they stopped and picked up a banana cream pie and a bottle of red wine. Richard answered the door and welcomed them inside. Richard introduced his wife, Melissa, to them, a beautiful brunette, much younger than Richard. She asked Barbara if she would like to have a tour of the house. "I would love to see it", said Barbara. The girls seemed to hit it off.

Chapter XXXVI

After a tour of the house, the girls got back to the living room and Richard asked them what they would like to drink. Barbara said, "Wine please". Steve asked for a beer. Richard went into the kitchen, while Barbara and Melissa chatted. Melissa said that she worked at a bank near the house, and Barbara said that she was a lawyer, working with her Dad. "Oh, said Melissa. "Maybe you can do our will". "Fine", said Barbara. "Come over to the office any time". Barbara gave Melissa her card and said, "Call me anytime".

Richard had a pool table in his den, and after dinner the time was spent shooting pool. At 9:00 p.m. Steve and Barbara said it was time to get home. They had a great time and invited Richard and Melissa to their home. On the way home, they both agreed that Richard and Melissa were nice and easy to talk to. "I like them", said Barbara. "They sure have good taste in furniture".

It may have been the wine and beer, but they both were tired and went to bed without putting on the TV.

Steve was up early, showered, shaved and getting dressed. Barbara was just getting up when Steve was making the coffee. "Morning, Barb", he said. "A little tired this morning, aren't we"? "Oh, morning, honey. I guess it must have been the wine". "Well, I've got to go to work, but you relax today and have a good day". Steve was gone, going to the bakery for rolls. Steve got to the station 20 minutes earlier than usual because the traffic was very light and he made almost every light. Rich came about 10 minutes later, said hello, and the two of them went to the squad room for the usual morning meeting. They were on their way, sitting in the squad car when Steve told Richard that they had a nice time at Richard's house, and Barbara enjoyed Melissa's company. She hoped they could do it again soon. "We will", said Richard. "Melissa liked you guys". They headed for an avenue that was reported of speeders by neighbors in the vicinity. They parked their squad car off on a side street so not to be seen when cars moved past the avenue. They were there five minutes when the first speeder went by. "Let's go, Rich", cried Steve, and off they went, light on and siren blaring. They caught up to the speeder in two short blocks. They told the driver to move to the right and park the car. The speeder moved to the right, parked, awaiting the officer to come to his vehicle. Steve got out of the car, approaching from the left. Richard moved to the car on the right side. Steve told the driver to roll down the window, which he did, and then told him to take out his license and registration. "What did I do?" asked the driver. "You have a real problem if you don't know what you did", said Steve. "You were going 20 miles over the speed limit, he said. Seeing that Steve had everything under control, Rich walked back to the squad car and called in the speeder's license plate number to see if there were any outstanding warrants out on him. In minutes, the radio came back on with no violations to report. "Thank you", said Rich. He walked back to Steve who was already writing out the ticket. "He's clean", said Rich. Steve handed the speeder the ticket and told him to slow down. "I don't want to pull you over again, OK?" "Fine", said the speeder and left. Steve and Rich went back to look for more speeders.

After giving out tickets to six drivers, they said they would call it a morning and head out for lunch, when a car shot past them, going over 60 mph. "Let's go", said Steve. They followed the speeder for four miles with lights flashing and siren blaring. He wasn't slowing down; instead he kept hitting the gas. The speeder was passing slower cars on the road, and Steve suggested calling in and getting a roadblock up ahead. "No", Rich said, "we will have him within the next mile or so". Steve did get on the radio and called in that they were in pursuit of a speeder. Finally, after two more miles, the speeder slowed down and let Rich get directly behind him, telling him to pull over to the side of the road. They noticed a woman passenger in the car, and figured the driver was showing off to impress her. The car moved to the side of the road and stopped. "I'll go and talk to them", said Rich, "while you call in the license number to see if he has any prior arrests". "OK", said Steve. Rich got out of the car and slowly approached the car. He noticed the girl turning her head to look at him. "She was so young", he thought. "Pretty, too".

As Rich was walking toward the car, he didn't notice the driver moving his arm behind him and grasping a 22 caliber pistol. "Kill him", said the girl, smiling. Rich noticed how young the driver was when he told him to open the window. The driver did as he was told and cracked open the window, just enough to raise the pistol and aimed it right at Rich. Rich, seeing the gun, Rich jumped to his left when he saw the gun being aimed at him and went to pull out his revolver. He saw the flash and felt the pain in his shoulder as he went down to the pavement. Steve saw his partner go down and grabbed the radio, yelling out "Officer down, need help"! He pulled out his gun and scrambled out of the car, firing two shots through the back window at the shooter. The shooter was hit in the back and dropped his gun. The young girl screamed when she saw the blood gushing out of her friend's mouth but picked up his gun. Steve rushed to the driver's side and pulled it open, and the shooter fell out at this feet. The young girl raised the gun and fired at Steve, hitting him in his thigh. Steve went down to his knees and fired once, hitting the girl in the side. The squad cars started to arrive, and the officers ran with guns drawn to Steve's and Rich's aid. Two ambulances pulled up next and rushed Steve and Rich inside for the drive to the hospital. The shooter and the girl were put in the second ambulance and they were also taken to the hospital. The shooter died, the young girl lived, surviving her wound.

Chapter XXXVII

The emergency room checked Steve's leg and determined that the bullet was lodged in his upper thigh and would need to be operated on to remove the bullet, since it was next to an artery. The doctor in the ER stopped the bleeding and had him removed to the operating room.

Rich's wife, Melissa, was notified, as was Barbara, and they both arrived at the hospital within minutes of each other. When they saw each other in the waiting room, they both hugged and started to cry. No information was given to either wife on the condition of Steve and Rich, only to say they are both in the operating room.

The hours passed slowly. Melissa and Barbara didn't say much to each other, just stared at the door, waiting for someone to come tell them how their husbands were. "What's taking them so long?" said Melissa. "I don't know", said Barbara. Barbara got up and said, "Let me go check with the nurse again". She went to the admitting desk and said, "Is there any word on our husbands?" "No", said the nurse. The doctor will be down to talk to you as soon as he can. Barbara went back to sit down next to Melissa. "Nothing", said Barbara.

The door to the emergency room opened and a young doctor came out and walked to Barbara and Melissa. The women got up and said, "Is there any news on our husbands?" "We just finished operating on Steve and Rich", said the doctor. "They are both stable, but not out of the woods yet". He looked at Melissa and said, "Are you Mrs. Deegan?" "Yes", said Melissa. "Your husband was shot in the armpit and the bullet exited out his back. No vital organs were hit, and he should have a full recovery". He looked at Barbara and said, "Your husband was shot in the thigh, and the bullet severed an artery. We gave him a blood transfusion and removed the bullet. He, too, will have a full recovery, but will need physical therapy to gain full mobility of his leg".

"When can I see my husband", cried Melissa. "You both can go up in about an hour, after they are assigned rooms". The women hugged each other, relieved that their husbands are alive and will be OK. They both started to sob in each other's arms.

Chapter XXXVIII

Barbara went to the phone, dialed her parents' home, and when Rose answered, she cried out, "Steve is OK. I'll be able to see him in an hour". Melissa called her parents to tell them that Rich is going to be OK.

Steve and Rich were put in the same room, both a little groggy, but thankful to be alive. Barbara and Melissa walked into their room and found them both sleeping. They both sat down in the chairs next to their husbands and held their hands. They both stared at them for what seemed hours, but was only minutes. They both held back tears. Steve was the first to open his eyes and saw Barbara looking down at him. "Hi Barbie", he said. "Hi honey", was Barbara's answer. She got up from the chair and gave Steve a kiss on the lips. Rich was given more anesthesia in the operating room and it took him longer to come out of it. When he did open his eyes, Melissa was right there looking down at him. "Hi honey", he moaned. "Hi yourself", said Melissa. "I love you".

The head nurse walked in and told the women that the doctor wants their husbands to get some rest, which is the best medication. Barbara and Melissa agreed and said their good-byes, and said that they would return later in the evening. Steve and Rich both nodded and threw kissed to their wives. Melissa and Barbara said their good-byes in the parking lot of the hospital, hugged one another and headed for their cars.

When Barbara got home, she was greeted by her Mom, who gave her a hug and asked how Steve was doing. "The doctor said that he will be OK but will need therapy to regain his mobility". "Is Steve's partner OK?" asked Rose. "Yes', said Barbara. "He should make a full recovery". "Thank God", said Mary. Frank saw Mary pull up and asked Barbara the same thing. Barbara finally broke down and said, "Oh God. He could have been killed". "He didn't", said Rose. "He will be OK".

After dinner, Barbara, Rose and Frank went to the hospital to visit Steve. Donny, Donna, John and Mary were already in the room. They all hugged and sat around the bed. Rich's parents and Melissa's were also in the room and chairs were hard to find. "Visiting hours are over", the loudspeaker blared. Chairs were moved around, most of them out of the room. The families said their good-byes and left.

Barbara and Melissa went back to their husbands, trying to get more time with them. After 15 more minutes, the nurse walked in and said that they would have to leave; medications are being given out. "OK", they said, and went to their husbands for a good night kiss. "Love you, Hon', said Barbara. "See you tomorrow". "With God's help", said Steve, and gave her a hug. The girls left together and Melissa asked Barbara to stop in a diner for coffee. "OK", said Barbara and followed her to the diner. The girls ordered coffee and pie and talked for an hour. They enjoyed each other's company, especially since the husbands were partners and together were sharing a room in the hospital. Barbara and Melissa said their good-byes in the diner parking lot and went their separate ways home. Melissa went straight to bed when she got home. Barbara talked to her mother on the phone for a half hour. She finally went to bed, but tossed and turned for a long time, blaming the coffee. She finally dozed off, thinking about Steve, a smile on her face.

Donny was getting tired of traveling into the city each day. He was seriously thinking of changing jobs but wasn't sure what he wanted to do. Steve told him to think of becoming a police officer. "Good pension", he told Donny. "Something to think about", said Donny.

The police test was coming up in two months, and Donny put in for it. He was getting out of the Navy in one month, and taking this test was falling in line with the plans. He had no intention of re-enlisting; that was going to be behind him.

Steve was briefing Donny on the police work and remembering more of the questions from the test, which would be changed for the time he took it. Donny took the test with several hundred other applicants. It was a long test, and when he finished, he wasn't sure how he did. "Time will tell", he said.

Months passed and Donny was discharged from the Navy, awaiting news from the police officer test. Each day Donny would wait for the mail to arrive, rush out to the mailbox to see if the results of the test were there. It took two months before the test results came. Donny nervously opened the letter. He tore the envelope opened and quickly checked the contents. He passed with a high score. He called Donna immediately to give her the good news. "I passed, I passed", yelled Donny. "Great", said Donna. "What now?" "I have to go for a physical and an agility test". "What is that"? asked Donna. "You have to pass an exercise test", said Donny.

Donny went for his physical and agility test two weeks later. There were many guys in the gym. He took a number and waited. The first test was to run 500 yards around the gym with a pack on your back and a belt with a meter on it. Donny had a bad left leg, which he used a cane for several months to keep his balance. He felt good after he got rid of the cane and exercised his leg daily. When his number was called, he got up, put on his pack and belt and was told to run. He ran at a slower pace than the rest of the guys, his leg bothered him some. He finished, took off the pack and belt and went to sit down on the bench. Next was climbing over a 6' fence. He got over the fence in a short time. The instructor told him, "Good job". Next they had to push an 80 lb. restraint across the gym floor. 'So far so good", thought Donny. Next was to pull a 175 lb. Dummy 50 feet. Donny threw the dummy across his shoulder and carried it the 50 feet. Laughter and clapping was heard. They now had to pull the trigger on a revolver 15 times with each hand. Sit-ups, pushups and chin-ups were done, and then came the physical. Donny finally found out how tall and how much he weighed. 5'11" and 160 lbs. He was glad this day was over. Now he waits to hear when he will go to the academy for six months and then his new career will start. "It's exciting", he thought. He called Donna as soon as he got home.

Rose was taking her pain medication daily, and when she stopped, the headaches started to return. "Oh no", she said. Back to the doctor's she went. She figured that she couldn't continue to live on pain pills. They left her feeling groggy. She made an appointment and saw the doctor a few days later. He told her that she would have to go for tests at the hospital. It could be a tumor, which he would like to rule out. Rose said she didn't want to go to the hospital, but the doctor talked her into going.

"Good morning, boys", said the nurse who walked into Rich and Steve's room. It was 8:00 a.m. Rich and Steve had their breakfast and were all washed and wide awake. The nurse had a therapist with her, a young girl who didn't look more than a teenager. They both went past Steve's bed and headed to Rich's side of the room. "We are here to get you up and walking", said the nurse. "Are you ready?" "I hope so", said Rich. "I'll give it my best shot". They positioned Rich to the edge of the bed, got on either side of him, and helped him get to his feet. He wasn't steady at all, but the nurse and therapist held him up. "Let's just stand here and catch our breath", said the nurse.

Rich was very unsteady and felt like he was going to fall over. "You won't fall', said the therapist, who put a cloth belt around Rich's waist. After what seemed like a long time, the therapist said, "OK, Rich, let's take that first step. Left foot out and don't be afraid; I have you". Rich took a step forward and almost fell over. "Hold it", said the nurse. "Get your balance and try again". He moved his left foot forward and followed with his right foot. "Great", said the therapist. "Now, let's try it again", "OK for now; let's head back to the bed", said the nurse.

Barbara had a busy day – two clients plus a closing and two wills. She went to the hospital in the evening with Donna to visit Steve. "Hi babe", said Steve when Barbara came in the door. "I saw you in the parking lot, parking the car. The nurse and a therapist came in and walked Rich today", said Steve. "I guess I will be next. It will good to get out of this bed and go to the bathroom by myself". Donna told Steve about Donny passing his tests and that he's now waiting for his date to start the academy. "He said he will be here later tonight", said Donna. "Great", said Steve.

The head nurse walked in, said hello and told Steve that he will be going down to the gym after breakfast tomorrow to start his therapy. "Great", said Steve. "I'm ready".

Chapter XXXIX

Donny walked in, gave Steve a handshake and started to tell him about passing the written and agility test and that he's ready to start the academy. He asked Steve what he will learn in the academy, and for the next half hour the girls listened to shop talk. "We might as well go down to the cafeteria for coffee", said Barbara. "No", said Steve. "We are done talking shop. Call me tomorrow, Donny, and we will talk more about the academy", said Steve. "Will do", said Donny.

Steve had his breakfast, washed up and sat in bed waiting for the therapist to come in and take him to the gym. He didn't have long to wait. In came a young skinny girl who didn't look anything like she could hold anyone up. "Hi", she said, stopping at Steve's bed and looking at the sign in front of Steve's bed. "You must be Steve", she said. "I'm Karen, your therapist from today until you walk out of this hospital on your own". "Hi", said Steve. "Are you ready to get going", she said. "I sure am", said Steve. She maneuvered the wheelchair to the side of the bed and said, "Let's get you in the wheelchair and get going". Steve slid his legs over to the side of the bed and positioned himself near the wheelchair. She told him to put one hand on the arm of the chair and she would help him get up and slide him in. She said, "At the count of three we will move. One, two, three", she said and lifted him up. With Steve gripping the arm of the chair, he lifted himself right into the chair. "Good", she said. Steve felt exhausted just from that little maneuver. She noticed him breathing heavily and told him to relax and enjoy the ride to the gym.

As she wheeled him in the hallway, Steve was looking around. He saw the nursery where all the babies were and was amazed at how small some of them were. When they got to the elevator, Karen pushed the button down. In a few seconds, the elevator came and the doors opened. She rolled Steve in and Steve jokingly said, "Down please". Karen smiled and said, "You are in a good mood, Steve". "Yes", said Steve. "I can't wait to get started". Karen pushed the button for the first floor and down they went. In a few seconds the door opened and Karen wheeled Steve out and headed for the gym.

As Karen wheeled Steve into the gym, he glanced all around, taking in the parallel bars, the stairs, and even a car at the end of the gym. On both sides of the gym was a row of people in wheelchairs, going through all sorts of exercises. Karen headed Steve to the parallel bars a wooden structure with hand rails on both sides. She parked the wheelchair in front of the unit and told Steve that she wanted him to get hold of both rails and pull himself up. She put a felt belt around his waist, which would help her balance him. He looked her up and down and said, "You think you can hold me up?" "Believe me, Steve, I can and will". "OK", he said. "At the count of three, Steve, pull yourself up. One , two, three". Karen got a hold of the belt and with Steve pulling himself up on the rails, he got up. "It felt good", he said "OK", Karen said. "Now, rest up for a minute and then we'll take a step forward". When she felt Steve was rested, she told him to move his left leg forward, taking one step only. Then move his left leg forward like she asked him to. Then she said to bring his right leg even with his left leg. He felt some pain doing that, but did it. "Now try it again", said Karen, "Left and then right". Steve did it with ease, within any pain. "Again", Karen said. "Try to walk to the end'. Steve did and then felt weak. Karen told him to hold on while she brought the wheelchair over. Steve was happy to sit down in the chair and rest. "We will sit here and rest for ten minutes", said Karen, "and then do it again". "OK", said Steve.

They continued the walking for the rest of the morning, and Steve was getting exhausted. "That's it for now", said Karen. "Let's get you back to your room so you can rest and have lunch". Steve was happy to get back to his room. Rich greeted him with "How did it go, Steve?" "Fine", said Steve, "but tiring".

After lunch Barbara came to visit with Donna. He told them about his first day of walking and about Karen. The next morning was the same. Karen came in, wheeling the wheelchair and parked it on the side of the bed. "Morning, Steve", said Karen. "Are you ready?" "Sure thing" said Steve, and maneuvered himself to the edge of the bed, got a hold of the wheelchair and lifted himself into it. Karen was surprised with his arm strength. "Very good Steve", said Karen, "but from now on, wait until I tell you to lift yourself into the wheelchair. I don't want any accidents". "Sorry", said Steve. "I will wait for your command from now on".

Karen wheeled Steve to the elevator and then down to the gym. A few of the patients who saw him yesterday said hello to him as he came in. "Nice, friendly people", he said, as Karen agreed. Today Steve was given a walker. Karen told him that she wanted him to get a hold of the walker with both hands while she helped him get up. "One, two, three", she said, as Steve got up, holding onto the walker. "Get your balance, " she said.

Once Steve got steady on his feet, Karen told him to push the walker slowly and take a step forward. He did as he was told, and proceeded to take steps across the gym floor, pushing the walker forward. Karen was in back of him, holding the belt to steady him. "Very good, Steve", she said. "Now try to walk clear to the end of the gym. "I'll try", he said, and proceeded onward, step-by-step. Patients sitting in their wheelchairs waved him on. Steve was getting the hang of it and started going faster. "Slow down", said Karen. "Right ", said Steve, and slowed down to a normal walk. He made it to the far end of the gym, and Karen came over with his wheelchair and told him to sit and relax for five minutes and try again.

After five minutes Karen had Steve get up and walk back to the other side. Steve felt good walking. He made it to the end without getting tired. Karen was there with the wheelchair, telling him to sit down. Karen let him rest for ten minutes while she went to her desk in front of the gym. When she got back, she wheeled him over to the wooden steps. "you will now get up, grab the railings and climb the stairs to the top. Once up on the deck you will rest for a minute and then come down on the other side. "OK," said Steve.

Steve got up when he was told, grabbed the railing and proceeded up the stairs very slowly. When he got to the top deck, he stopped and rested while looking around the gym. After he rested, he started down the steps and found it much easier coming down. When he got to the bottom, he heard applause from two patients sitting below. "Thanks", he said. Karen asked him to do it again, and he said OK.

After a brief rest, Karen wheeled him to the car that was a shell of a car with doors. She told Steve to open the front door and try to sit on the front seat, grasping the steering wheel for support. He had no problem getting in and sitting in the front. "Great," said Karen. "Now let's try the other side". He again got in with little effort. Karen told him to relax for a minute and then she wanted him to use the walker and walk back to his room. "Do you want to try it?" she said.

"Yes," said Steve. She told him to get up and get going. Steve grasped the walker and started walking with Karen holding the belt behind him for support. He walked to the elevator, pressed the button going up and when the doors opened, he got in. "Very good", said Karen. He got out of the elevator, made a left in the hallway and walked into this room. "You look great", said Rich. "I feel great," said Steve, and headed for his bed.

Ted and Jennie were now looking for a house near John and Mary. They saw a For Sale sign on a nice three-story home only two blocks away on a side street. They told John and Mary about it and asked them to go with them to look at it that evening. "Fine", said John. "It will be good to have you guys as neighbors". Ted called the number on the sign and made an appointment with the owner to look at it that evening.

The four of them took the short walk to the house and rang the front doorbell. A man in his 60's opened the door and welcomed them in. The man's wife who was also in her 60's told Jennie the house had two bedrooms on the first floor with two bathrooms. The upper floor was the same as their apartment. The basement was remodeled and had one bedroom, a bathroom and an eat-in kitchen. It was now rented to a nice young couple. Jennie loved the place and in minutes after looking around, told Ted, "I want this house". The grounds were manicured with two cherry trees on the side of the house. There were three sheds in the back yard. In the front of the basement was a large coal burner, which was converted to oil.

After touring the whole house, Ted said, "We will buy it. "The rent income will pay our mortgage', said Ted. Jennie was all excited about buying the house. Ted had a good job as a reporter for the Polish newspaper. He only had one had habit: he enjoyed playing the horses and would go visit the racetrack two times a week. He never told Jennie when he lost, but bragged when he won with a dinner celebration. They had a few dollars saved up, but Ted slowly used that up. Jennie never realized that he was using the savings for gambling because Ted handled all the bills.

Chapter XL

Rose entered the hospital a few days later with Frank at her side. Barbara told her that she would go visit her that evening. Rose felt uneasy and wanted to cry, but Frank told her that she is there for tests, nothing else. "Who is going to cook for you?" said Rose. "Don't worry your pretty head about that. We will survive. We will all pitch in a cook and take care of ourselves. I want you to stop worrying about us; rest and do like the doctors say". "Oh, OK", said Rose, trying to smile for him.

The hospital started taking rests in the afternoon. Rose felt like a pin cushion, with the nurses coming in and taking blood samples. X-rays and scans were taken and the day went by quickly. Rose didn't have time to think about her condition. Pain pills were given to her whenever she requested them. Barbara and Steve went to visit her that evening, driving in with Frank and Donna.

The doctor came into Rose's room the next day and told her the tests showed a small tumor, which could be taken care of. "You will need an operation which a neurosurgeon will remove the tumor. You will stay in the hospital for seven days and then go home where you will rest for a few weeks, forgetting about housework for that period of time and heal. You should be as good as new after that". He made Rose feel at ease, like it was a simple operation. It was far from a simple operation, but why worry her anymore than she already is.

When the family came in the evening, Rose broke the news to them. It hit Frank pretty hard, but she tried to do her best to reassure him that it's for the best, and the doctor feels that she will be good as new.

The neurosurgeon came into visit Rose a day later, explaining to her what had to be done. He told Rose that he does this operation five or six times a week, making Rose feel at ease. "We will have to shave those beautiful curls on one side, but your hair and curls will come back in no time flat. "When will you operate?" asked Rose. "Well, I have two operations to take care of, but can schedule you in this Friday morning. Let's get it done and over with, Rose", he said. "Fine", said Rose. "Friday it is". In her own mind, she thought maybe he would operate in a week.

Chapter XLI

Oh well, the sooner the better. Rose would stay in the hospital, going through all tests, X-rays and finally be prepped for Friday morning. No sense in going home for a couple of days and then come back.

Friday morning came. She was given a light breakfast and was ready. The nurse came in, prepped her, and gave her a mild tranquilizer. They wheeled her to the operating room at 10:00 a.m. Frank was there with her since 8:30 a.m. Barbara would go to the hospital at noon, hoping the operation was over and her Mom was doing well. Steve told her that he would take off from work if she wanted him to go with her. Barbara told him no, that she would call him after the operation was over.

Joe and Eleanor were planning a trip to Florida to see how their home they bought was coming along. They asked john and Mary to come with them and fly to Florida instead of driving. "Maybe next time", said John. He was busy with three orders to make fur coats, plus he was behind on his cleaning. Joe and Eleanor understood and said that they would take pictures of their home to show how far they were in building. Mary told Eleanor that they will spend their retirement years with them.

Joe and Eleanor bought themselves a Golden Retriever puppy that was very gentle. They asked John and Mary to watch the dog who was called Summer. They bought him in the summer so the name was perfect.

Whenever Joe and Eleanor came to visit John downstairs, Summer was right there and getting acquainted with John and Mary. John told Mary that they don't have to get a dog; they have Summer who they see every day and give him treats.

John told Joe and Eleanor that he would drive them to the airport. Eleanor told him that their flight leaves at 9:00 a.m. and they would have to be at the airport two hours before the flight leaves, which would be 7:00 a.m. "No problem", said John. We will leave here at 6:30 a.m. and that will give us plenty of time to get to the airport. We shouldn't hit much traffic at that time. Let us know what time your flight comes in back to Midway Airport and the flight number, and I will be there to pick you up and drive you home". "Are you sure, John?" said Eleanor. "Positive", said John. "It will be nice to have

Summer for a week. He is a good watchdog". "That he is", said Joe. "While in Florida we will talk to the builder and find out when they plan to finish our homes. We will call you if they have any questions, like the colors of the tile and paint". "Great", said John.

Rose was operated on and the surgeon removed the tumor, which was smaller than they anticipated. Rose spent two hours in recovery and asked the doctor when she will be able to go home. "In about ten days", said the doctor. "Let's not rush it". "OK", said Rose, groggy but happy it was over.

Frank, sitting in the waiting room, was informed that the operation was over and she was in recovery. He could go up and see her for a short time before she goes into an assigned room. When Frank walked over to Rose in recovery, a nurse was taking her blood pressure. Rose was semi awake and when she saw Frank, a big smile came to her face. "Hi honey", he said. "Hi sweetheart", said Rose. "The doctor told me everything went well and you were a fine trouper. You should be assigned a room in an hour or so". "Good", said Rose. "You look tired, Frank", said Rose. "Why not go home and take a nap and come back tonight". "In a little while", said Frank. "You look beat, honey, seeing what you went through." "I'm glad it's over, Frank. I think I will rest now and say a few prayers to thank God for looking over us". "I haven't stopped praying since you came to this hospital", said Frank.

Ten days later, Rose was told that she could go home, and that everything is great. They removed the whole tumor and she should be as good as new in a couple of weeks. "Oh, great", said Rose. "Let me call my husband and have him pick me up". She dialed the number and Frank answered. "Hello, honey", she cried. "The doctor was just here and said that I can go home this afternoon. Please come over and pick me up, OK?" "Why certainly, babe. I will be there in a few minutes". "OK", said Rose.

Frank cleaned up the kitchen and ran the vacuum so the place would look nice. Rose keeps the place spotless and yells at Frank when he doesn't pick up after himself. He was on the way in minutes, happy that Rose would be home soon.

When he walked into her room, she was all dressed and sitting on the bed, her small suitcase all packed next to her. "Hi, Hon", said

Rose. "All set"? asked Frank. "Yep", said Rose. "Let's go home". The nurse wheeled Rose to the front entrance while Frank pulled the car in front. Rose got in and they were on the way home.

John set his alarm clock for 5:00 a.m. He didn't want to oversleep today, taking Joe and Eleanor to the airport. John is usually an early riser, but he wanted to make sure he got up early. The alarm woke John at 5:00 a.m. He showered, shaved, dressed and put on the coffee. He was on his second cup when Joe and Eleanor came down to let him know that they were all ready if he was.

"Good morning, Joe and Eleanor", said John. Just then Mary waked into the kitchen and said, "Good morning". She was in her bathrobe. "Go back to bed", said Eleanor. "Later; I had to get up to say goodbye to you guys. Have a great trip and call us whenever you can". "We sure will", said Eleanor. "Now let's get going".

Traffic was light going to the airport. They took the highway straight to Midway airport. They got to the airport at 6:40 a.m. He parked the car and they walked to the entrance. They said their good-byes at the entrance door, and Joe and Eleanor went inside. John headed back to the car.

Chapter XLII

Ted was on a losing streak and figured he would quit playing the horses after one big win. He went to the woman who handled his pension at work and borrowed money from it. One big win and that is it he kept telling himself.

One day Jennie got a letter from his job, showing how much he had in his pension. Jennie was shocked to see the withdrawals. When Ted got home, she was waiting, and before he sat down to talk to her, she threw the letter at him and gave him both barrels. "What are you trying to do to us", she cried. "You are using up our retirement nest egg. I want a divorce", she said. Ted didn't know what to say, except he started to cry and said that his gambling was out of control. He knew it and said that if she forgave him, he would never gamble again. She loved Ted and said OK, but if you ever do this again, that will be it. They hugged and cried together.

Ted got paid twice a month and was paid in cash. Jennie decided that to make sure Ted didn't get the urge to play the horses, she got a ride to the paper twice a month and picked up his pay envelope. Ted wasn't happy with her doing this, but he ignored it and gave her the envelope whenever he got paid. Jennie took over paying the bills, too, and always gave Ted his allowance of $20.00 per week. She figured that was more than enough to last him from payday to payday. Jennie never brought the gambling up again. If he has money left over from the $20.00, she figured he can bet on the horses. They seemed closer to each other than ever. Both were happy now.

Eventually, Ted stopped playing the horses and never bought the race form again. She got Ted interested in gardening, landscaping, and even a vegetable garden, which he was proud of. He enjoyed watching his tomatoes grow. He got to bragging about how big his tomatoes are and he thought he had a green thumb. He gave tomatoes and other vegetables to the neighbors, who really appreciated it. They bought a freezer and put it in the garage so Ted could freeze his vegetables, and they ate them all year.

Chapter XLIII

Rich was going home. He mended quickly and Steve was happy for him. "I'll be going home in a few days", said Steve. "I can't wait." Rich was all dressed when Melissa entered the room. "Hi guys", she said. Rich got up, walked over the Steve and said, "I'll be seeing you soon, partner". "Sooner than you think", Steve said. "As soon as I get home, we will get together and have a few beers". "Right on", said Rich, and he gave Steve a hug. Rich's wheelchair came and as he was wheeled out of the room, he gave Steve a thumbs up sign.

Barbara and Donna came that afternoon and saw Rich's bed empty. "Did Rich go home?" asked Barbara. "Yes, just a short time ago." Karen walked in as the girls were there, and Steve said to Barbara, "Why not come to the gym and watch me work." "OK", they said and Karen wheeled Steve to the elevator with the girls behind them. Karen started Steve on the steps, which he did well, then a walk around the gym with the walker. Barbara was really proud of Steve, and kept waving to him. Karen told Steve to sit in the wheelchair and rest while she went to her desk. She came back a few minutes later and in her hand was a cane. "You graduated to a cane, Steve. Now let's see how you do." Steve got up, got his balance and moved freely with the cane. It felt good to him.

When Donny took the police test, there were over 4000 applicants and he scored 925th with a score of 91%. He was contacted 6 1/2 months after he took the test to start the Academy. He was happy but nervous at the same time. When Donny entered the Academy, it was the scariest day of his life. It was hopefully the best day of his life career-wise. The first day he entered in professional attire, which was worn for the first two weeks. This was because they eliminate candidates at a rate of two recruits a day during this period. This eliminates the police from retrieving police equipment from terminated recruits. The first four weeks the staff Sergeant tries to break them down, both mentally and physically in order to build the recruits up to their liking.

The entire Academy stay is seven months. The staff treats the recruits as if they want them to drop out, which some do. The second month Donny was bombarded with intense law information and physical and mental challenges. Each week Donny had an academic test which grew each week to incorporate the prior week's information. There were also four major tests through the Academy stay and the final exam. The third month Donny learned first aid and other safety issues.

Donny passed his physical agility test with no problem. Others who failed this had to spend two extra hours a day working on their faults. The fourth month of the Academy Donny was sent to a specialized unit for intense training. Donny was sent to water survival that consisted of going to a large public pool and swimming a dozen laps. To Donny who was a Frogman, this was a snap. They had to put on a winter dry suit that made them look like Gumby swimming in the water. While in the water for ten minutes, they have to take off their uniform and belt and be able to use the uniform as a personal flotation device by tying the pant legs and blowing air into them and then using them as floats. The same thing was done with the shirt.

Donny then went to EVOC class, Emergency Vehicle Operating class. This simply was the ability to operate a patrol car under emergency conditions. The vehicle is driven at high speeds around obstacles. Donny thought this part of the recruit training was fun. He got to drive the patrol car at amazing speeds and push it to the limit in order to get to know its abilities of the patrol car. This included spinning out of control on the wet pavement and going through tight spaces at high speeds.

Donny next went to FTU, Firearms Training. Donny was taught how to strip the weapon and how to maintain it. He was taught how to fire the weapon and be accurate at the same time. A majority of police weapon discharges occur within ten feet of the perpetrator, and 90% of them occurring within ten yards. Donny was then sent to Hogan's Alley, which is an enclosed course that simulates pop-up targets with women and children among the bad guys. He had to eliminate the proper threat. Donny didn't do too well at first, but he got extra hours of training and came to be a good judge of who to shoot at.

Donny thought the next course was boring and almost unnecessary. It was called a cultural diversity course. He was taught that people are equal, no matter what walk of life, and that some cultures don't like the police and can't accept them with open arms. They attempt to thicken your skin while throwing racial and ethnic slurs around the room. This has important, in that if a person calls an officer a racial slur, it is a violation, but if they call a police officer a racial slur, it is merely angry speaking. The police officer has to have a thick skin.

Chapter XLIV

Riot control was next and was simply a one-day course with the mounted unit. Donny learned crowd formation and direction.

Traffic control was next and probably the most senseless of the courses. Most people with general knowledge of the vehicle and traffic laws understand and obey the traffic laws.

After Donny completed the Academy classes and specialized training, he went out in the field called Field Training. Donny went out into the real world with a specialized officer assigned to him. The recruit works the same hours as the training officer. The training officer lets the recruit do all the paperwork while being monitored. The hearing officer fills out a performance sheet for every day worked on how the recruit performed that day, as well as how they dressed and dealt with the public. The recruit is also monitored on how he drove and directed traffic.

Graduation day was the most exciting day of Donny's life. "The day before graduating, he got to call the people who taught him for seven months by their first names instead of Officer Smith. Donny felt strange to say Hi John, when for seven months it was Officer John. It is then that he realized it was all a game. They broke you down and then brought you back to life. They made you realize that you are part of a brotherhood, a brotherhood that no one will realize unless they've gone through this living hell. Donny said it was one of the worst experiences he endured, but it was definitely a rewarding one.

Ted and Jennie's day of moving to their new home finally came. Donny and Donna were there to help, as was John and Mary. A couple who lived next door came over and offered to help them move. Their names were Linda and Rob. Rob is an electrician, working in a college nearby. Linda is a nurse, working for a doctor two blocks away. She could make a lot more money working in the hospital, but chose to work for this doctor, James Pawlerowski. It was nice to walk to work. She had her bachelor's degree and was now working on her master's degree in the evenings. They were doing very well with two salaries coming in. They bought a half-acre of land in Somerset Lake, an hour drive from them. They bought the half-acre with the idea of building a home for their retirement. In the summer months they tried to make a few trips to the lake. Rob liked to fish and caught a two-foot Musky off the docks last year. They purchased a small boat, a little bigger than a canoe, with a small motor on it. They liked riding the lake and looking at some of the homes on the lake. They had a ford pickup truck with they offered Ted and Jennie to help them move. "Great", said Ted. "My brother-in-law, Jim, is coming over with his pickup truck, too."

Ted and Jennie's apartment was just a few blocks from their new home, so they didn't have far to move. Jim came with his truck and the moving started. The biggest item was a piano that everyone agreed to move out first. John was right there with the younger men, directing the piano through the doors. It didn't take long and the piano was in their den. The bedroom sets were next and the dressers emptied to move them easier. In a few hours they were finished. They took a beer break and sat in the kitchen talking about how much is remaining to do. They still had the beds to put together and small odds and ends. When they finished, Linda came over with a pan of Ziti. Everyone was starved by then and waited for the Ziti to be ready. Jennie brought out paper plates. Dinner was delicious and the full pan of Ziti was gone. Out came a delicious apple pie that was bought while the move was on. Coffee and apple pie went great after dinner.

Ted hooked up the washer and stove. He was handy that way. Rob checked the electric circuits and all electric receptacles for frays and overloads. They were done. Ted thanked them all.

Steve was getting to walk very well. Karen figured it would be soon and he goes home. He started walking without the cane a short distance, then a little longer. He climbed the stairs very fast and came down the same way. "He definitely should go home", said Karen. She made out her report that evening, and recommended Steve be discharged. There was nothing more she could do. She did recommend a therapist to visit Steve at home for seven weeks. She told Steve that she recommended for him to be discharged, and he felt like crying with joy. "OK", he said.

Chapter XLV

Barbara came to visit him in the evening and Steve gave her the good news. "I should be going home in a day or so", he said. "Great", said Barbara, and walked over to him and gave him a big kiss. The next morning the doctor walked into Steve's room and told him he could go home. He signed the papers releasing Steve. Steve called Barbara and said, "Pick me up, Hon. I'm going home".

Frank and Barbara had to work a lot of hours lately, and the backload was at a point where they had to give up some cases to other lawyers. Rose pitched in and did a lot of the typing for both of them. They even had to hire a typist part time to keep up with the load. The young girl who just finished her junior year in high school was a fast and accurate typist named Casey. She was 17 and a conscientious worker, coming to the office after school, on Saturdays, and even Sundays. Casey was doing a lot of dating before coming to work for Frank. She had to curb her dating while working. She enjoyed making money and was smart enough to know that she couldn't go out every night and work, too.

Frank and Rose decided that they needed a vacation or get burned out, so after taking care of the big cases, they called their friends in Daytona Beach who they knew for years. Frank went to law school with Frank Balinski. He like being called BO, which all of his friends called him. Bo got on the phone with Frank and welcomed them to come visit them. Bo and his wife, Rita, were both lawyers and did well in their business. They stayed friends since law school and entertained together. "OK", said Frank. "We will call you when we decide on the date". "Fine", said Bo.

That evening at dinner, Frank asked Barbara to come with them to Daytona. "I would love to", said Barbara, "but now with Steve home and him getting therapy at home, I couldn't. "Well, talk it over with Steve and let us know. That goes for you, too, Donna", said Rose. "Let me think about it", said Donna.

Chapter XLVI

When Barbara got home she mentioned to Steve that her parents were going to Florida and she and Donna were asked to go with them. "I told them that I couldn't go with you being home and needed my help". "Honey" said Steve, "call them and tell them that you can go with them. I want you to go Hon" said Steve. "I can manage by myself for a week. I'll eat at my parents' house, so call them and say yes Barbara. You need to relax". "Okay" said Barbara, if you think you will be okay". "I'll be just fine Barbara." "I'll call you everyday from Florida to see how you are doing, okay?" "Fine" said Steve.

Barbara called her mom and said, "Hi mom, Steve told me to go with you guys. It will do me good. Let me know when you and dad are leaving, and if Donna is going, okay?" "That's great" said Rose, "and yes, Donna called and said that she can go. We plan on leaving a week from today". "Great" said Barbara. "I'll stop over tomorrow morning and get all the information. We can talk about the clothes that we should bring". "Fine" said Rose. "I'm glad you girls are going".

Barbara was excited about going, but she wished Steve was going too. She called Donna and the two of them sounded like two schoolgirls. "It should be fun" said Donna. "Yeah" said Barbara. "I think we should go clothes shopping soon". "How about tomorrow". Said Donna, "is that soon enough?" They both giggled.

Barbara and Donna went to their parents home the next morning to get information about the trip. Frank said that they should leave around 7:00 am to beat the traffic and get a jump on it. "It should take us around 18 hours" said Frank, "Stopping one night in a motel. We have enough drivers to do this". Everyone agreed on the day and the time. Frank called Bo and Rita in Florida and told them that they were coming to Florida and that they should come see them while they are there. "Great" said Bo. "It will be great to see you all. Rita will be all excited about you guys coming".

Packing was done during the week. They were all set to leave on the day they planned. Steve and Donny waved goodbye to them until they were out of sight. They both wished they were going.

Chapter XLVII

After driving for 6 hours straight Frank said "I'm pulling into the next rest stop so we can all stretch our legs, go to the bathroom and get something to eat". All three of the girls said great. It was 3:00 pm in the afternoon and hungry they were. Frank pulled into the rest area, found a parking spot near the entrance to the restaurant and parked.

Everyone got out and headed for the bathroom. They all ordered hamburgers and shakes and sat down to eat. "We are a quarter way there," said Frank. "How about letting me drive for awhile," said Barbara. "Fine with me" said Frank.

After lunch they got gas and were on the way. Barbara drove for 5 hours and Frank said "how about we pull in a rest stop for dinner and then try to find a motel for the night". "Great" said Rose.

They got off an exit that said hotel, restaurant two miles ahead. Frank directed Barbara looking for the motel. They saw the sign Howard Johnson's – Rooms and Restaurant. Barbara pulled in. They had a big dinner, talked and then got two rooms for the night.

They left the next morning after breakfast, all rested. Frank then took over the driving. They passed through South Carolina, and in a few hours were going through Jacksonville. They parked the car at the sign that said "Orange Juice", got some juice from the stand and continued on.

They got to Daytona late in the afternoon and found Joe and El's house with no problem. They pulled into the driveway and out came Joe and El running to meet them.

The next morning everyone walked to the beach. The temperature outside was 90°. The girls ran to the water, which was warm. They dove in and swam to a raft that was anchored 50 feet away. Rose, Frank, Joe and El all followed and got on the raft. "It is beautiful here", said Rose. "You guys should retire here", said Joe.

Chapter XLVIII

Barbara dove into the water and started swimming away from the raft when she suddenly felt something hit her upper leg. "Shark!" she yelled. She reached down to her leg expecting the worst, but everything seemed okay. She started swimming as fast as she could toward the raft, getting to the raft in seconds. Joe and Frank pulled her up, asking if she was all right. She looked down at her leg and said "I'm okay, just a little shook up".

Barbara swam to the beach and in shallow water she started to run for the sand. When she got on the beach she sat down in the sand and started to massage her leg, which was now a deep red. It looked like a red rash. Joe and El got to her and said that something rammed into her, maybe a shark or a jellyfish. "No more water for me today", said Barbara. After 10 minutes she got up, a little weak, but got her balance, and said that she would like to sit on the beach near the walkway. Frank helped her with Joe on the other side and she sat on the beach, shaken up a little. "Wow", she said, "I wonder what that was that got me?" "Looks like a big jellyfish", said Joe. "A shark wouldn't leave a make like that". Barbara sat on the beach for the rest of the day while the rest of the family swam, staying in the shallow water. They would come over and check on Barbara every so often. She kept telling them that she was okay. They didn't stay long, figuring that Barbara would be better off sitting on a soft couch, with her leg up, so they packing up and drove back to the house. Joe's patio was all screened in and had two couches in it, which Barbara sat in one with her leg up.

Donna and Barbara got back from their trip in time for Donny's graduation. The sore on her leg was clearing up, just a little discoloration, which did not bother her. Donny was notified that the academy ceremony would take place in two days. Before the ceremony there is a Final Inspection. Drill sergeants and class leaders line you up military style and give one final inspection before accepting you as one of theirs. This process takes 1½ hours standing at attention while these distinguished members of the force inspect every square inch of your attire and posture. They do this one by one and nobody is excused until the last recruit is inspected. The day of Donny's graduation was on a hot steamy day. Standing outside in this uniform felt as if it was dripping off him.

Chapter XLVIX

After the inspection, Donny was sent back inside with the rest of the recruits and they were given their assignments (which precinct they were going to respond to and what squad you were in). Donny was all excited to find out were he was going to work. After this, Donny was sent to a large hall, where family and friends gathered for the promotion ceremony.

Donny didn't realize that this ceremony would be such a long and dragged out process where they let everybody who thought they were important to society say their peace and congratulate themselves on putting this class together. The Mayor was there to make his speech and near the end he mentioned and said "We have a Medal of Honor recipient in the class, I would like to have him stand up". Donny stood up to a tremendous applause.

After graduation was over Donny responded to his appropriate precinct for a two-hour interview with the precinct commanding officer. He welcomed Donny and gave him a quick run down on the operations of the precinct. Donny was then handed off to the precinct clerk who gave him a map and some essential police forms that he would need on his first day of patrol. The forms included accident forms, tickets, alarm forms, etc. He was then sent on his way.

The first day of his tour Donny called the precinct and was told where he was to meet the officer that he was relieving. To Donny it was the scariest moment in his life. When Donny met the Patrolman he was relieving he gave Donny the keys to the car and the portable radio and said to have a safe day. Donny didn't have a partner as of yet, so he wondered what would he do if he got a call.

After driving around for a while and not hearing any tangible words from the radio, just a lot of squabbling, then it happened. He heard his car number to respond to a disturbance. His jaw dropped and he got butterflies in his stomach. He responded to the call and settled the husband/wife squabble. It felt pretty good to get through his first call that easy. After a couple more minor calls Donny's shift ended. He went home and told Donna about his exciting day.

Donny was working 12-hour days, plus an hour to and from work. He needed his sleep and went to bed early. After a few days Donny was getting comfortable responding to the call. He was getting confident in this ability to diffuse situations.

Donny was patrolling the streets for a few weeks now and was getting the experience he needed. It seemed to come easy for him. Donny was told that he may be getting a partner soon. New recruits were at the academy now and soon may come to the precinct after graduation. The crime rate in the city was increasing and it needed more police officers.

After patrolling one neighborhood, Donny got a call about an apartment building fire and to proceed to the area to direct traffic. When he got to the street he could see the smoke coming from the apartment building on the corner of the street. No fire trucks arrived as yet, so he parked his car a block from the area and proceeded on foot to the building. When he got fifty feet from the building he noticed a screaming woman from a second floor window. The window was open and she was half out of it. Smoke was pouring out but he couldn't see any flames. "Help", she cried. She was holding on to the sides of the window trying to get air to fill her lungs. The smoke was billowing out of the window. Donny had to act fast. "Get out on the ledge and jump, I'll catch you", he yelled. "Don't be afraid. Jump like you would into a pool", he yelled, "feet first". She was terrified but did as Donny told her, jumping feet first. Donny braced himself and caught the force of the impact of her in his left side. He grasped her in his arms and landed on the grass. He never let go of the girl. She landed on top of him, knocking the wind out of him. He regained himself and looked at the girl who was sobbing "My brother is still in his room" she said, pointing to the window upstairs. "He is in his crib". Donny now jumped to his feet and ran to the door hoping that it was open. He got to the door, grabbed the knob and turned it. The door opened and he looked up the stairs to his left through the white, thick smoke, which was getting thicker. He took a deep breath and ran inside, taking the steps two at a time. He didn't see any flames yet, just smoke. The fire must be in front of the building he thought.

When he got to the top of the stairs he heard the baby crying. He half crawled to the sound of the boy, who was still in his crib. He picked up the child and ran back to the stairs, taking two at a time. His lungs were bursting now as he bolted out the door, jumping down the three steps to the ground. He laid the boy down on the grass and tried to get up when just then two uniformed fire fighters came to his aid and the baby. "Took in a lot of smoke", said Donny. One firefighter picked up the child and ran to the fire truck to get the oxygen mask and applied it to the baby. The young girl was up and aware when Donny talked to her. She told him "thank you for saving our lives". Donny was happy she was okay and the baby boy will be fine he was told.

Donny started to cough and a fireman brought over an oxygen mask for him. "I'm okay" he said. After fifteen minutes Donny felt good enough to go and do what he was called up to do, direct traffic.

The fire was put out in an hour, and when the fire trucks left Donny walked over to his car and headed back to the precinct to make out his report. The sergeant at the precinct told Donny to stay in the precinct and do other paper work for the rest of the day. He noticed that Donny was more than usual, and probably needed a rest.

When Donny got home he told Donna about his exciting day. "Are you okay Donny" she asked. "A little sore, but yes, I'm okay". After dinner Donny and Donna relaxed and watched a baseball game at a park near their home.

Steve told Donny that he was going to put together a ball team and join the league at the park. Donny said "Count me in Steve, I'm all for that". The softball league at Kos park was played with sixteen inch softballs. No gloves were used. Steve and Rich were now back in the patrol cars patrolling the streets once again. "It sure feels good to be back at work" said Rich. "Yeah", said Steve "I was starting to get bored laying around.

Chapter L

He told Rich about the softball league and asked Rich if he wanted to play. "Sure" said Rich. "I played a lot of years ago. I caught and played second base" he said.

Steve asked a few other guys at the precinct and after a few days of looking and asking he finally got ten players for his team. In softball it takes ten players, a short center makes the tenth player in softball. He played directly behind second base.

After a shift was over Steve took a ride to the park to sign up his team. The team would be called the Ridgelawns. Some of the players came from Ridgelawn, some from Haborlake.

The organizers of the league told him that he would be getting a softball schedule in the mail when the league secretary marks one up. Steve called Donny and told him about signing up the team to play at the park and Donny told him that he heard that there are some good teams playing in that league. "Not as good as our team", said Steve. They both laughed.

A few days passed and Steve received the baseball schedules. His first game would be in two weeks. Barbara spoke to her father about sponsoring Steve's team. The advertisement on the jerseys would be better than advertising in the paper. Frank thought it over and agreed to sponsor the team. The full uniform for 10 players, plus two substitutes. They picked the color of the blue pants and white jerseys. The cap would be blue with an "R" insignia. All the information was given to the factory including the sizes. The woman at the factory told them that the uniforms would be ready in four weeks. They would have to play the first two games without the uniforms.

Steve had practice three times a week in the evening when everyone was home from work. He also called practices on the weekend. He told the team they have to be ready for the first game.

Chapter LI

On the day of the first game, they all met on the north side of the field by home plate. Showed up waiting for Steve to come with a line up. People were gathering on the grass and around the field to watch the game. Steve finally came and called out the names of the ten players who will play in today's game. Two of the players had to sit on the bench hoping that they will get a chance to play. The umpires arrived and were given the line up of both teams. The umpires called Steve and the other team captain to home plate for the coin toss to see who will bat first. Steve called Heads but Tails came up. The other team chose to bat first. Every one of the players on the other team had on green uniforms that looked impressive. Steve's team had tee shirts and jeans, all mixed. Steve called out for his team to take the field. Donny played first base and Steve will pitch the first game. The new eleven-inch ball was thrown out to Steve who took a few quick pitches and then threw the ball to the third baseman for a little practice. The ball was hard when new. By the end of the game the ball will become soft. The winning team gets the ball. The first man up hit a ground ball to the short stop, who picked it up and threw it to Donny for the out. The next two batters hit fly balls to the outfield and the first part of the inning was over. Steve's team came to bat.

Donny was the first to bat on his team and hit a ground ball to second for an easy out. The next two batters popped up in the infield and the inning was over. The next two innings were the same, with no one getting a hit.

Donny came up again and hit the first pitch over the first baseman's head. He ran to first and glanced to see the right fielder chasing the ball, so he took off for second base and got there easily. The ball went to third base and held Donny up on second. The next batter was Stanley, a good friend of Steve's and one of the best hitters on the team. He hit the first pitch, a line drive out to center field. When the ball was caught, Donny tagged up and went to third base. Getting on third. Now it was one out and a man on third. Wally came up next, the short stop who Steve called Blondie. The ball was hit on the second pitch between Short and Short Center. Donny scored easily and the short center threw the ball into the dirt at first. Blondie went to second as the ball got away from the first baseman. The next batter was Tom who everyone called the Ox. He was built like a guard on a football team. He was Donny's neighbor. Tom waited until he got two strikes and then hit the ball, straight up. It took a minute for the ball to come down and was caught by the pitcher. Steve's team was up by one run and it stayed that way until the eighth inning when the green team got up.

The first batter got a hit, driving the ball over the second baseman's head. Steve yelled out double play guys. The next batter hit a slow dribbler down the first base line, with Donny charging the ball. As he picked it up he was off balance and threw it over the second baseman's head. It was picked up but the center fielder who threw it to third, but not in time for the out. They now had a man on first and third, no outs. "Let's settle down: yelled Steve. The next batter hit a fly ball to left field which was caught and the runner on third scored, tying the game. The next batter hit a grounder to Stanley, who threw it to second, getting a forced out and then to Donny and got a double play. Was retired, bit the score was tied.

The score stayed tied until the end of the ninth inning when Steve's team came up. Stanley came up and grounded out to third base. Blondie was up next and waited out the first two pitches. The next pitch was his, chest high, he hit the ball dead on, out to right field. It went over the right fielder's head, past the people sitting on the grass and rolled up to the children's pool. Blondie ran around the bases like he was being chased, and when he touched home plate a roar came from the crowd. They won the first game and were hungry to have done so.

Steve got the team together and he said "we were lucky to win today. I hope you all realize it. We played sloppy and came out winners." Donny spoke up and said "I was the only sloppy one on the field. I rushed that grounder when I should have let that ball come to me". "I think we were all a little sloppy", said Steve. "We will improve. I'm sure of it", he said.

"The next game was scheduled in two days. We won't have our uniforms yet, but we have to win. We are playing the Blue Hawks who won big today. I know a few of the players on the team and we are in for a tough game". "Anyone for going for a beer at John's Tavern"? Half the guys said sure and to the tavern they went.

The owner at Jon's Tavern was happy to see the guys patronize his tavern. He told them that we would sponsor the team if they couldn't find anyone else, but Frank was happy to do it for Steve. The guys had a pitcher of beer and left calling it a day.

Steve and Rich were back to patrolling the streets of Chicago. They both had some aches and pains, but that will soon pass they thought. They got a call on a family dispute, a short distance from where they were. They approached the small ranch and rang the bell. A woman, bleeding from the nose, answered the door and told Steve and Rich to come in. "Thank God you're here", she said. "He wants to kill me". They looked around the living room, which was spotless and well taken care of. The furniture looked new and they had a large TV in the corner of the room. "Where is your husband", Steve asked. "He is in the bedroom, he locked himself in when I told him that I called you". Rich went to the bedroom and knocked on the door. "Does he own a gun", Steve asked the woman. "No", she said. "He does have a shot gun that the uses for duck hunting, but that is in the closet in the hallway". Steve opened the closet and saw the shotgun in the corner of the room. "What is your husbands name", asked Rich. "Ron" she said. "The husband told Rich to go away. It's a family matter and we don't need you" he cried out from the bedroom. "Come on out, we just want to talk to you", said Rich. The doorknob turned and the door opened. Ron stuck his head out of the bedroom and saw Steve and Rich standing a few feet from the door. Neither man made a move toward Ron. They waited for him to come out, which he did. "I'm not a criminal", Ron said. "My wife hit me with a pot and I just hit her back. End of story", he said. Steve questioned the wife and she told him that Ron was abusive to her so she hit him with the pot. Steve and Ron got together and agreed not to take the husband to the precinct. The couple looked like they had a squabble, they both lost their tempers. It seemed like it was over. The wife didn't want her husband in jail. Steve made out the report and told Ron and his wife to kiss and make up, which they did. They told them to think twice before you call us again, because the next time one of you will to go jail. Steve and Rich seemed satisfied and left. "I don't think they will call us anymore," said Rich.

They went back to the patrol car and by now it was lunchtime. "How about a hamburger", said Rich. "Fine with me", said Steve.

They stopped at a fast food restaurant and ordered hamburgers and shakes. While at the restaurant they talked about the softball game they had yesterday evening. "We have a good team," said Steve. "Just need a lot of practice." "I agree with you", said Rich "about the practice". "Ha ha", said Steve. They went ahead and ate and Rich said "OK Steve, let's get back to keeping the peace".

Busia's birthday was coming soon, she was turning 90. Mary was planning on going shopping with Jennie and Eleanor for Busia's gift, and asked Busia to go with them to pick out her gift. Busia said she felt tired and felt like she was getting a cold, so the three of them went. Mary bought Busia the dress she was looking at the last time they were shopping in that store. Eleanor got her perfume which Busia likes and Jennie got her a purse. After shopping in many stores, they went to lunch and talked about having a small party for Busia with some of the neighbors coming over. "Sounds like fun", said Jennie. After visiting a few more stores they decided to call it a day. The three of them were tired from all that walking. It took them a few minutes to find the car with all the cars in the parking lot. Eleanor said that it would be a good idea to draw a map next time to find the car. They all laughed.

They hit a lot of traffic on the way home and couldn't figure out why, until they came upon an accident a mile ahead. They saw a few patrol cars and an ambulance ahead. As they passed the accident they noticed someone being put on a stretcher. "I hate to see an accident", said Mary, "it makes me nervous to drive home".

Mary dropped off Jennie and Eleanor and then proceeded home. When Mary opened her kitchen door, she didn't see Busia, who she thought would be having a cup of tea around this time. She went to Busia's bedroom and was surprised to see her still in bed. She usually took a short nap and then would start supper. She dropped off her packages and then called out to Busia to let her know that she was home. She got no response from Busia. She entered the bedroom and called out to her again but Busia didn't answer. She died in her sleep. She screamed for John, who heard her and rushed to her side. Nothing could be done for Busia. John called the doctor, whose office was on the next block. The doctor came right over, checked Busia and said that Busia's old heart just gave out.

Mary, John, Jennie and Ted went to the funeral home to make the arrangements. Mary brought the dress she got her for her birthday and told the director that that was the dress she wanted Busia to be laid out in. "I want Busia to meet Dziadzi in that dress. At the wake Eleanor put the perfume in the casket. Busia was buried on her 90th birthday. "Our Queen was buried today", said John.

Everyone on the softball team showed up for the second game of the season. Steve came with the line up and called out today's players. Ox would pitch while Steve played second. The catcher was Tyler, the youngest of the team members. He was a fireman in the city and lived two doors from Steve. Steve never saw him hit a ball, but he was a part time weight instructor and had a muscular build. He told Steve that he played softball with the fireman team. He said that he couldn't play every game, because his work schedule prevented him from doing so. "Okay", said Steve. "We have Tom to play when you can't".

The Blue Hawks gathered near third base and looked impressive with their navy blue uniforms. Steve's team won the coin toss and chose to have the Blue Hawks bat first. The ox was warming up when Steve called for the team to get out on the field. The Ox then pitched a few pitches to Tyler and said he was ready.

The Ox, being nervous, walked the first batter. Steve walked over to Tom and told him to settle down. The next man hit a fly ball to center field, which was caught easily. The man on first decided not to try for second. The next man up hit the ball over the right fielders head, and ended up against the fence by the children's pool. The ball was retrieved by the right fielder and thrown to Steve, who threw it to Tyler at home. Both runs scored and the inning was just starting with one out. Steve walked over to Ox again and told him "No problem Ox, we will get those runs back. Settle down and get the next two outs". The next man hit a foul ball, which was caught by Stan at third. The next man hit a grounder to Blondie, who picked it up and threw to Donny for the third out.

Steve's team was up and Ox hit a grounder to third for an easy out. Next came Matt, who hit a line drive to left for the second out. Blondie was up next and beat out a grounder to short center. Steve got up and took two balls it looked like it would be over the right fielders head, but he ran a few feet back and caught the ball. No runs and no hits – still 2 to 0.

In the bottom of the ninth Steve's team was still down by two. "Let's go guys", yelled Steve. "This is it, now or never". Tyler got up and hit a ground ball to third, which was dropped by the first baseman. Tyler got to first base. Nick was up next and on the first pitch hit a line drive right at first base, which was caught. Tyler was half way to second. The first baseman stepped on first for a double play. "Oh nuts", yelled the team. Donny got up and grounded out for the third and final out. The blue Hawks rejoiced while Steve's team sulked. "We lost", said Steve, "It's bound to happen. We have to win next week. Practice tomorrow, right guys"? No celebration today, everyone took off their spikes and said goodbye and went home.

When Steve got home he took a hot shower, grabbed a beer and went into the living room and sat down. He put the TV on but couldn't concentrate on it. His mind was on the game that they lost. They weren't better than us he thought, we just didn't play good enough to win.

Barbara had to work late again, and when she got home she saw Steve sulking on the couch. "How did the game go Steve", asked Barbara. "We lost Hon, but could have won if we played better". "Did you pitch" asked Barbara. "No, I let Ox pitch. Tyler showed up today and I let him catch. I played second base". "How did Ox pitch"? "Good he was a little rusty in the first inning, and one guy belted the ball to the fence by the pool for a home run". "Wow", said Barbara. "After that inning Ox settled down and pitched a good game. We weren't hitting today, or we would have beat them", said Steve.

Steve got a call from the uniform factory telling him that the uniforms were ready for pick up. The next day, after an easy day at work, Steve drove down to the factory and picked up the uniforms. He had time before going home for dinner, so he delivered the uniforms to his team.

Everyone showed up at the park wearing the new uniforms. Steve was impressed when he showed up with the line up. "We look real sharp", he said, "now let's beat the pants off the White Shirts".

Tyler had to work so Ox caught and Steve pitched. They lost the coin toss and went first to bat. Donny led off and after two bad pitches hit the ball, a line drive over the third baseman's head. The left fielder was playing shallow and had to go chase the ball. Donny rounded first and stopped at second base. "All right" yelled Steve, "let's keep the ball rolling and bring Donny around to home". Joshua was up to bat and hit a slow grounder to short center that the pitcher couldn't reach. Donny went to third and Joshua got to first base. Stanley came up and hit a lone drive over the left fielders head, scoring Donny and Joshua. By the time the left fielder retrieved the ball, which was near the tennis court, Stanley scored easily. His second home run to date. By the time the inning ended, Steve's team was leading 5-0. The game ended with Steve's team wining 8-0. It was time to celebrate.

Donny and Donna stopped over to see Steve and Barbara and talked about taking a trip to Riverview, an amusement park across the street from Wrigley Field. All rides on Tuesday and Thursday were 2 cents, which was a good price. They decided to go on Thursday, when Steve and Donny had a day off. It doesn't happen very often that both of them were off on the same day.

When they got to Riverview the line for admission were a half block long. Donny didn't care for roller coaster rides and Steve like them but didn't like the whip and rides that spun around. The girls enjoyed all the rides. One ride that everyone enjoyed was the Parachute Drop. They all headed for that ride first, the lines were long at all times. When they got to that ride they found only three people ahead of them, so they went and purchased the tickets. As you went up you could see the whole park, even Wrigley Field. "The Cubs must be in town", said Donny, "look at that crowd". When they hit the top they were released and floated down, catching the warm wind. "Wow", said Donna, "that was fun". They continued to walk around the park and went on most of the rides. The bumper cars had a line two blocks long, but they waited. Finally they got into their cars. Donna and Donny made a pact to catch Steve in the corner and ram him. "Ouch", he yelled, "no fair – two against one".

After they left the amusement park they went looking for a restaurant so neither of the girls would have to cook that night. "That's so sweet of you guys", said Barbara. Traffic was heavy, due to the Cubs baseball game, but they finally found a nice Italian restaurant on Belmont Avenue. Steve found a parking space right in the front of the restaurant. When they got out of the car they could smell the Italian cooking. "I'm getting hungry", said Steve. "Me too", was Donny's comment. They all ordered veal cutlet Parmesan, which was the special of the day.

Steve said that they should go to the Polish restaurant in Niles one day. It was across the street from the cemetery. "The food is out of this world", said Steve. "Now that Busia is gone they don't get to eat too much kielbasa, except on Easter. Donny said "How about next weekend"? "I'm for that", said Steve, "you girls agree"? "Sure", said Barbara and Donna. "Anytime we don't have to cook is great". "Okay", said Steve, "next week it is".

Chapter LII

They left the restaurant and found the traffic a little lighter. They put the radio on and listened to the Cubs game.

Steve and Rich were patrolling the south side of Chicago when they got a call to proceed to the bank on Lake Avenue. A silent alarm was triggered, proceed with caution, the radio said.

When they got to the bank everything seemed normal, normal from where they parked the car. They could see the bank from where they parked. Rich shut off the engine and said "Looks peaceful to me. Maybe the alarm was hit by accident". "Right", said Steve, "let's go and check'. They saw people going into the bank but no one was coming out. As they got out of the car a shot rang out from the direction of the bank and hit the windshield of the car, missing both of them by a foot. They both got down and crawled behind the car for protection. Rich crawled to the drivers side, got to the radio and called for assistance. "Shot fire", he blurted out. They both pulled out their revolvers and watched the front entrance of the bank. Two squad cars arrived, sirens blaring, parked near Steve and Rich. A Sergeant crept toward them and asked what was going on. "Have you seen any movement inside the bank"? "No", said Rich, "just one shot fired from the side door", pointing to it. "It hit our windshield", said Steve. The Sergeant told them to keep an eye on the front door while he went to his car to get a megaphone. He got in position behind his car and called out to the thieves in the bank. "you in the bank, the bank is surrounded and you can't get out. Let all the people in the bank out. We will give you two minutes to comply". The bank door opened and two shots rang out, hitting the squad car that the sergeant was behind. Steve and Rich, seeing the bank door open, open fired, filing six shots at the bandits. The door closed before Steve and Rich could get off any more shots. The front door opened a crack and the thief inside yelled that they have six hostages inside, plus the bank manager and four clerks. "If you fire another shot at us you will get a dead hostage". The Sergeant yelled out to his men to hold their fire. "No more shooting". "Now the waiting begins", said Rich. The Sergeant got on the radio and called for the SWAT team. There was no communication between the thieves and the police for over a half hour. The SWAT team arrived in two vans. They scrambled out all dressed in protection clothing. Another car showed up. An FBI agent stepped out and walked over to the Sergeant. "My name is Joshua Johnson, FBI", he said. "I will take charge now". No one argued, in fact he was relieved. He brought Joshua up to date on the shooting. Joshua had told the Sergeant that he put a sharp shooter on top of the roof opposite the bank. He had put another two doors away from the first shooter. Both sharp shooters had portable radios so they could communicate with Joshua. Once the sharpshooters were in position Joshua asked them if they could spot any of the thieves. "No" was the reply. The blinds of the bank were shut. Joshua picked up the megaphone and began to talk. "You in the bank, this is the FBI. We don't want to see anyone get hurt. We advise you to release your hostages and come out with hands above your head". The back door opened just enough to see an arm with a gun in it fire off two shots at the man with the megaphone. The shots went wild and penetrated the door of a car. Joshua went to his knees and told the sharpshooters to take a shot at any thief that they see. The door closed before any police opened fired.

Joshua was getting annoyed. He told sarge "I guess we will have to remove them". Joshua ordered tear gas to be shot into the front window of the bank. With the SWAT team going in the front and side doors. "I want everyone to get into position", he said. "Once we go in, watch out for hostages. Yell to them to hit the floor".

Joshua called the bank from the phone that was set up for him. He got Bob on the phone, he was head of the thieves. "This is Joshua, head of the FBI. You know you can't come out of this bank alive, so why don't you release the hostages and save yourselves". "Listen Joshua", Bob said, "If anyone tries to enter the bank we will kill all of the hostages". If you shoot tear gas in the window they will all die. Do you read me Josh"? "Okay", said Joshua, "what is it you want"? "I want you to remove those guys across the street with the rifles, that's number one. Next, I want a helicopter put down in the parking lot." "Hold on", Joshua said, "I don't know if I can get a helicopter here". "Well", Bob said, "if you don't have a helicopter in the parking lot in one hour I will kill one hostage. One per hour after that if I don't see a helicopter here". He then slammed down the phone. Joshua could see what he was up against and called out to remove the sharpshooters. He then called FBI headquarters and made a report to the head man there. "We need a helicopter here really quick", he said, "or they will start to kill the hostages". "Okay", said the man, "I'll call you right back".

Joshua didn't have to wait long, the phone rang. "Josh?" "Yes". "This is Bill, we will have a helicopter in the parking lot in a few minutes. We have an agent flying it and he will be armed. You have to take the robbers before they get to the helicopter. Don't let us down Josh".

Josh called the bank and asked for Bob. "Yeah", said Bob. "The helicopter is on its way. It should be here shortly". "Fine", said Bob. They hung up the phone.

Josh started working on his plan to place agents and police around the side of the bank and around some of the cars in the parking lot. He had several cars in the parking lot removed so that the helicopter could land. He would have the helicopter surrounded and take the thieves down before they could board the copter.

The helicopter landed just where Josh told him to. One agent was in the helicopter. Josh called the bank and Bob picked up the phone on the first ring. "I see it Josh", Bob said. "Make sure no one is near it when we come out. Remember Josh, we will have hostages around us".

Bob got his two accomplices and told the four hostages to get over by the front door. Bob looked out the window and couldn't see any police around. He told one of the thieves to carry the satchel with the money in it and said "we all go out together. Walk toward the helicopter. Keep the hostages close to us. When we get to the helicopter check to see if anyone, besides the pilot, is in it. We back off if we see anyone in the helicopter, keeping the hostages close. They opened the door, looked out and slowly moved out. They all stayed together, with the four hostages, two in front and one on each side of them. As they got closer to the helicopter Joshua made a motion to wait.

Chapter LIII

Steve and Rich huddled in the same spot since they got to the bank. They kept watching the back door of the bank. Now they were watching the three thieves and four hostages. Neither one would ever have a clean shot at them. Twenty feet from the helicopter the pilot pulled out a revolver. He opened the helicopter door yelling for the thieves to drop their guns. Joshua gave the order to move in ten men from the SWAT team, four FBI agents and a few policemen moved in on the robbers. Guns drawn Bob panicked when he saw the agent in the helicopter and the police rush in on them. "We give up", cried Bob. "Don't shoot. He dropped his gun and the agent jumped from the helicopter and got to Bob and the two thieves in seconds. "On the ground", he ordered them. The FBI agents, SWAT team and policemen went to help and handcuffed the culprits. Joshua moved in and ordered the thieves into a paddy wagon for a ride to the jail. "Good job", he told them all.

Joshua called his boss at FBI Headquarters and told him that everything was under control and that the culprits were on their way to the station. The hostages are all OK and will take a ride to the station to make out the reports.

Steve and Rich called it a day, went to the station, made out their reports and went home.

Donny had a peaceful day, no serious calls. He heard about the robbery at the bank when he got back to the station to sign out. The Sergeant told Donny "Your brother had an exciting day today Donny". When Donny got home he told; Donna what he heard about Steve at the bank. She immediately called Barbara to see if she heard from Steve. Barbara told her that Steve called and said he is fine that that he and Rich were at the Bank Robbery today. He said he had an interesting day watching the back door of the bank from behind his patrol car. That was it.

Seeing today was Friday and Donny was off on Saturday he asked Donna if she wanted to go out for dinner and then go visit Steve and Barbara. "I have chicken in the oven, but we can always eat it tomorrow. I wouldn't want to pass on the restaurant", she said with a smile. "Fine, give Barbara a call and tell her our plans". "Okay Donny", she said. Donna went into the kitchen and called Barbara to ask her if they would be home this evening because she and Donny would like to come over to visit. "Great", said Barbara, "Sounds good. We plan on staying home tonight anyway". Donna told Donny "Okay, they'll be home".

After dinner at a nice Italian restaurant they picked up a cake to bring to Steve and Barbara's house. "Hi guys", said Donny as he walked in the front door. "I hear you and Rich had a little episode at the bank today". "You heard already?" said Steve. "Happy endings travel fast", said Donny. "So, let's hear about it brother". "Yea", said Barbara, "Let's hear about it. All I got were dribs and drabs". Steve proceeded to tell them from the time they got the call until the robbers gave up, never mentioned the shot that hit the windshield. Barbara doesn't have to know about that he thought. After cake and coffee Donny told Steve about the two of them making a trip to Poland on their next vacation that they could get together. "That would be great", Steve said. "We can look up Tommy and his family while we are there. It would be nice to see our old house, if it's still standing". "Why not go to the travel agent one day or evening to check out the prices"? "Great", said Steve, "How about tomorrow evening"? "I'm Okay with that", said Donny. "How does going to Poland next month sound? I'm sure we both can get the time off".

Plans were in motion about the trip. Barbara and Donna were asked to go with them, but declined the invitation, maybe some day, but not right now. "I think the two of you should go and enjoy yourselves", said Barbara. Steve and Donny looked at each other and said "Let's go then"!

A few weeks went by and the vacation was planned for June. They got the time off, got the flight to Poland and were all set to go.

At the airport they picked up a coffee and roll and waited for the flight to be announced. By the time they finished their snack they were told to board. Steve took the seat by the window and told Donny that on the way back he could have the window seat. "Okay", said Donny and picked up a book to read, which was in back of the seat. "We will be flying over a lot of water", said Steve. "It will be good to know where the life jackets are". "Right", said Donny, "as if we would survive a plunge into the water". The trip was long and they both snoozed for some of the trip. They got sandwiches for lunch. Steve had a martini while Donny had a beer.

They landed in Warsaw the following day. It was beautiful, but still being worked on.

Steve and Donny got their luggage, called the cab which was right outside the terminal, and headed for the hotel. The hotel was new and clean. They were speaking in Polish, which they didn't forget. The next morning they went to the restaurant closest to the hotel and ordered breakfast in Polish. "Are you Americans"? asked the waitress. "We are now", said Steve. "We were born in a small town on the outskirts of Krakow". "Your Polish is good", said the waitress.

After breakfast they went to the train depot and bought tickets for their old town. It was a short ride on the train. They got off the train and were amazed to see the transformation of the old little town. They didn't recognize the town at all, nothing seemed the same. They caught a cab that went by and told the driver to go to the hardware store on Yeden Street, which Dziadzi owned. The street was still there, but the building wasn't. It was a parking lot now for some stores. They told the cabby to now proceed to the old house they lived in. It too was gone, and an apartment building was in the plot.

They went to Tommy's house, which was now a store. They asked the owner what became of Tommy and his family. He told them that he didn't know, but they could find out by going to the City Hall of records. They went there and got lucky and got Tommy's new address. They rang the bell and Tommy answered. He changed a lot, as they probably did. Tommy had a puzzled look on his face. They proceeded to tell Tommy that they were investigating a murder of a German soldier with green teeth. With this Steve went into laughter and couldn't stop. Tommy figured it out and burst into laughter also. He jugged Steve and Donny and started to cry. Now all three were crying. Tommy invited them to dinner. Tommy's parents were still living and were full of questions about America.

After dinner the boys took a walk to the lake. It looked much smaller now. The raft and spears were all gone, but the catfish was still in the lake, they were almost sure of it.

The tried to talk Tommy into coming to America but he said his life was here. The next day there were on their way to America, home sweet home. They weren't sad about leaving Poland. They made their home in America. They couldn't wait to get home and be with their wives, which they missed.

Barbara and Donna picked them up at the airport at Midway. They were all smiles as they got off the plane and into the arms of their wives.

They took a lot of pictures of the old town and what it was today. "Mom and Dad wouldn't recognize the place at all. It's all rebuilt", said Donny. "I couldn't believe it". They stopped at a restaurant near home and told their wives all about the trip. "I'm glad we went", said Steve, "but I don't want to leave America to go again". He squeezed Barbara's hand and she smiled.

Donny got to the station a half an hour early as he usually does so he could have his coffee and talk to his friends on the force. At 8:00 am he was called into the office. As he entered he noticed a young man of 19 or 20 standing at the officer's desk. "Come in Donny", said the Lieutenant. "You remember I mentioned to you that we would get you a partner some day, well the day is here. This is Ryan Sanling, your new partner. He doesn't live too far from you. Ryan this is Donny. Why don't you guys sit in the cafeteria for a half hour and get acquainted. After that, go out there and stop crime". They shook hands and left the room. Ryan asked Donny as they headed to the cafeteria "How long have you been on the force"? "A couple of months", said Donny, exaggerating a month or so. "Where do you live Ryan"? "On Milwaukee, near Western Avenue", he said. "Hey, maybe we can car pool once we get situated and get to know each other better'. "Sure", said Donny. Ryan was engaged to be married in two months. He told the Lieutenant he needed two weeks off at that time. The Lieutenant, an understanding married man, approved this and said "No problem Ryan". "Are you married"? asked Ryan. "Yes", said Donny, "almost six months now", again exaggerating a month or so. "No children yet", he said. After a brief discussion Donny said "Are you ready to roll"? Since Donny was the senior man, he had the option of driving or letting Ryan drive. "I'll drive", said Donny. They had the northwest side to patrol and Donny asked a lot of questions while he drove. "No calls all morning", said Ryan. "Is this a slow day"? "You'll welcome a slow day Ryan. Not long ago my brother, who is a cop, had a slow day and then all hell broke loose. They got a call for a bank robbery". "I read about it in the papers", said Ryan.

"Your brother was there"? "Yeah", said Donny. "They had a pretty rough time for a while, but the robbers panicked when an agent hid in the helicopter". "Wow", said Ryan. "Was he scared"? "You have to know my brother Steve to get the answer", he said. "He is a tough cop", Donny said. "I'll bet he is", said Ryan. "This lunch is on me, my initiation fee", said Ryan. "Okay partner" and Donny laughed.

They were getting along fine. Donny hopped Ryan would be a capable partner. They got their hero's, paid and ate in the squad car. "Boy, these hero's are great. Well worth the money", Ryan said. "Didn't I tell you that you would like them"? said Donny.

After lunch they started to patrol the neighborhood. A call came through and said a possible break in at a warehouse near Montrose Street. "Okay", said Donny, "action here we go". The sirens were blaring and Donny raced through the streets like a racecar driver. He slowed down slightly at intersections with lights, but then he hit the gas until he came to another light. The warehouse was huge and was a block long. Donny pulled up near the front door, and shut off the engine. "Let's go", Ryan called out. Donny went to the door and turned the knob. The door opened. Donny and Ryan froze. They drew their revolvers and paused. "Il just go in", said Donny, "cover me". It was dark in the warehouse and very quiet. Donny carefully waked in and once inside he tried to adjust to the dark room. He whispered to Ryan to bring the flashlight. Ryan went to the car, got the flashlight, checked to make sure that it worked, and went into the dark warehouse, moving very safely. He saw Donny against the wall and moved next to him. "See anything"? he whispered. "No", said Donny. "Let's slowly move to the center of the room". Just then Donny froze, as did Ryan. They heard voices up ahead. "Someone's up ahead", said Donny. With guns drawn they moved ahead. They saw a little light ahead and moved toward it. Someone was looking at the crates stored there with a flashlight. They moved in as close as they could and caught shadows of someone opening a crate with a crowbar. He told Ryan to flash the light in their direction, which he did. "All right, yelled Donny. "Drop the crowbar and put your hands up". "Don't shoot", came the sound from the one with the crowbar. He dropped the crowbar and kept yelling, "Don't shoot". Ryan and Donny approached the two figures and when they were a few feet from them Donny said, "kids, it kids". Ryan with a gun still drawn approached the two who had there hands raised and now were crying. "Get on your knees", yelled Ryan, who removed his handcuffs from his belt and put it on one of the kids. Donny did the same and hand cuffed the other. "Outside", he ordered the kids.

Once outside Donny and Ryan put them in the back seat of their patrol car and called in to say they are bringing in two kids caught in the warehouse. The warehouse is secured he said.

At the station they turned over the kids to a Sergeant who went to question them. Donny told Ryan "Good job", they could have had guns. "We did good". "Yeah", said Ryan "It was good". They were like two peas in a pod. They would be good as partners.

Melissa gave birth to a boy and named him Don. Donny was the Godfather, Donna the Godmother.

Chapter LIV

Donny retired from the police force and is currently writing a book on the US Seals, formally called the Frogmen. Donny and Donna have three sons, one of which is called Donny. Tommy never moved to the United States, he got married and has two daughters, named Barbara and Donna. He writes to Steve and Donny often and says he plans to make a trip to visit them soon.

ISBN 142515519-7